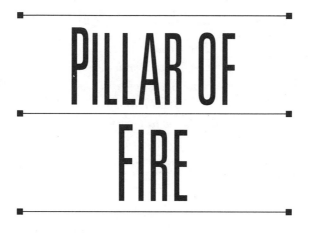

PILLAR OF
FIRE

PILLAR OF
FIRE

A Moroni Traveler Mystery

Robert Irvine

St. Martin's Press New York

Library of Congress Cataloging-in-Publication Data

Irvine, R. R. (Robert R.)
    Pillar of fire : a Moroni traveler mystery / Robert Irvine.
      p. cm.
    "A Thomas Dunne book"
    ISBN 0-312-13588-2
    1. Traveler, Moroni (Fictitious character)—Fiction.
I. Title.
PS3559.R65P55   1995   95-34733
813.54—dc20   CIP

First edition: December 1995
10 9 8 7 6 5 4 3 2 1

*The author wishes to thank Natalie Bowen
for making the journey.*

To Elisabeth Story
And to the memory of John Buettner-Janusch,
who helped me see Utah through fresh eyes

Pillar of Fire

ONE

A halo, some trick of the light, surrounded him like bridled fire. A foot-high platform, nothing more than raw pine planks crudely nailed together like a barker's soapbox, creaked beneath his shifting weight. Gusting wind flapped his shirttails as he stretched out his hands toward the crowd, which abruptly closed around the wooden stand as if reacting to a prearranged signal.

"If you came here expecting miracles," he told them, his voice rising, "leave now. I'm only a man, not a magician. God knows my failures outnumber my successes."

His hands fell, thumbs hooking into the pockets of his well-worn jeans, a cowboy's pose.

"You cured my son," a woman said.

"I comforted him. I spoke with him, but in the end he cured himself."

"You gave him medicine when all others said it was useless."

"I gave him hope."

Another woman fell on her knees, hands together in prayer,

eyes shining with gratitude. "My child also. You stole her back from death's door."

Shaking his head, the man raised his eyes to the red buttes that dominated the horizon. The soil, too, was red, and the sky, in contrast, seemed a painful blue beset with clouds shaped like white boulders.

The kneeling woman held up her child; the man beside her followed suit. "We ask to feel your touch, your blessing," they said in unison.

"Each will be seen in turn."

"Bless you," the crowd murmured.

Someone screamed. A woman, wild-eyed, hair as disheveled as Medusa's, leapt onto the platform, thrust a revolver hard against the man's chest, and fired. He stumbled backward a step before regaining enough balance to look down at his blackened shirt front. He touched what should have been a wound, then smiled to show he wasn't hurt. His lips moved. The words, lost in the tumult as the woman was knocked from the platform and subdued, could have been "I'm sorry."

The image froze. Josiah Ellsworth, apostle of the Mormon Church, fiddled with the remote control device in his hand, punching buttons until the television screen went black and the videotape ejected from the VCR on Moroni Traveler's desk.

"They say he's the messiah," Ellsworth said. "They say God's hand reached out and stopped the bullet."

Traveler said nothing.

"I'm told he walked out of the desert one day and began working miracles," Ellsworth added. He was a tall, bone-thin man, an inch or so below Traveler's height, dressed in a dark blue, almost black, suit, stark white shirt, and funereal tie.

"Does the man have a name?" Traveler asked.

"Jason Thurgood."

Traveler gestured at the blank screen. "Where was this taken?"

"Just outside Fire Creek, one of those old mining towns in the Furnace Mountains. It's what they call a home video and was taken by one of Thurgood's followers. Someone, a friend, had it dubbed for me."

He rose from the client chair in front of Traveler's desk, stepped to the door, and knocked on the frosted panel. Immediately, two men, the Tongan bodyguards who'd earlier carried in the TV equipment, retrieved the gear and departed.

As soon as their footsteps faded down the Chester Building's granite hallway, Ellsworth unfolded a map and pointed out Fire Creek in the extreme southwest corner of Utah, not far from the borders of Arizona and Nevada.

"That's cult country," the apostle said, running his finger along the state line. "Filled with would-be prophets claiming to have the ear of God. Polygamists mostly, who mistake hormones for piety."

"And Thurgood's one of them?"

Ellsworth returned to his chair, sat stiffly, steepled his fingers, and stared at Traveler. Traveler stared back, wondering at the man's motives. Being an apostle placed Ellsworth among the chosen twelve who advised the president of the Mormon Church, the living prophet. But there were those who said that Josiah Ellsworth was more than an apostle, that he was in fact the White Prophet, the head of the legendary Danites, the church's avenging angels since the days of Joseph Smith and Brigham Young.

"I knew Kary, your mother," Ellsworth said abruptly.

"In what sense?"

"Why is it I have the feeling that you expect me to answer 'In the biblical sense'?"

"In that case we might be related," Traveler said, knowing that a man like Ellsworth would certainly be aware that Traveler's legal father, Martin, had been off fighting a war when Traveler was conceived.

Ellsworth smiled, removed a white, crisply ironed handkerchief from his pocket, and wiped his brow, which looked perfectly dry. "You need air conditioning, young man."

"We usually get cross ventilation." Traveler indicated the office's two open windows.

"It's a hundred degrees outside, hot enough to turn the asphalt into chewing gum, and God knows what it is in this office," Ellsworth said. "And to answer your question, as far as I know Thurgood himself isn't a polygamist. He's not even a cult member."

Ellsworth reached into his coat pocket and extracted one of those self-sealing plastic sandwich bags, containing what looked like a black ball. "When I was a boy we rolled tar into balls and chewed it because there wasn't enough money for gum. On hot days like this, we'd dig it out of the road with our bare hands."

His perfectly manicured fingers, Traveler noticed, were far too clean for such a deed. No doubt his bodyguards had obliged.

Ellsworth broke the bag's seal and sniffed at the opening. "It brings back memories, I'll tell you. Childhood is such a wondrous time. Of course, these days you can't chew it, not knowing what's in it." He took a long deep breath. "Before I came here I was in the temple praying for guidance. When I stepped out into the heat, I looked across South Temple Street and saw the Chester Building and remembered your office. I took that as a sign I should come here."

Traveler clenched his teeth. "Does Willis Tanner have anything to do with this?"

"He recommends you highly, if that's what you mean. He's a loyal friend of yours, and has been since grade school, as I understand it."

Traveler nodded.

"One strayed," Ellsworth said. "The other took God's path."

"I know Willis speaks for Elton Woolley, the prophet, but does he speak for you too?"

Ellsworth's lips twitched, as if fighting a smile. "I wanted you to see the videotape for yourself before we talked. What do you think happened? Was it a miracle?''

"It could have been a blank cartridge in the gun, a setup.''

"Even as we speak, the woman who fired the shot is being held in jail at the county seat, charged with attempted murder.''

"Have you spoken with the police there?''

"Not personally, but I'm assured that the attempt was real enough. My sources say she doesn't deny it. In fact, from what I hear, she says she'd shoot Thurgood again if she ever gets the chance. Of course, the whole thing may be some kind of cult dispute, though the woman—she calls herself Sister Vonda Hillman by the way—is mute on that subject. As for the police, they say she's a member of a cult that calls itself *Moroni's Children*. From what I hear, the Children have run all the other cults into Arizona.''

Ellsworth resealed the sandwich bag and set it aside on Traveler's desk. "Not the kind of offspring a Moroni like yourself had in mind, I'm sure.''

"I still don't see what you want from me,'' Traveler said.

"If the gun was loaded, that would make it a miracle, wouldn't it?''

Traveler replayed the scene in his mind. Thurgood had been wearing a loose-fitting shirt. A flak jacket could have been concealed beneath it.

"I'm only a private investigator,'' he said.

" 'The Lord Omnipotent who reigneth, shall come down from heaven among the children of men, and shall dwell in a tabernacle of clay, and shall go forth amongst men, working mighty miracles, such as healing the sick.' ''

"Who has he healed?'' Traveler asked.

"That's why I'm here,'' Ellsworth said. "I want you to investigate him for me. Records show he's licensed to practice medicine in this state, but we can't find any indication that he's ever done so. I want you to find out the truth about him. Is he the fake I think he is, or something more? Is it possible that the messiah is among us?''

"No you don't. That's your area of expertise, not mine."

Ellsworth held up a hand. "A man in my position can't go poking around in a small town like Fire Creek, or even a rural county seat like St. George. In any case, if I send in one of my people, someone known to be connected with the church, word would get around that we take this man Thurgood seriously. The resulting publicity could be disastrous."

"Surely, you can't believe that he's anything but a do-gooder?" Traveler said. "At worst a charlatan."

"My daughter believes, that's enough. Her son, my grandson, who's named after me, has Hodgkin's disease. So far he hasn't responded to conventional medical treatment, which means he's going to die. So it's no wonder my Liz—Elisabeth Smoot's her married name—is willing to try anything. Acupuncture, Chinese herbs, or Jason Thurgood. Whatever works."

"Take him to Thurgood and be done with it. Even if he's a quack, it can't hurt the boy."

"She and young Josiah are with him now, living under God knows what kind of conditions."

"What do you expect me to do, play doubting Thomas and stick my finger in his wound to see if it's real?"

"If that's what it takes."

"What about your daughter's husband? Why can't he do your dirty work?"

"Surely you've heard of Orson Smoot?"

Traveler shook his head.

"My son-in-law is a theologian and church archeologist, and he's not yet forty. He's on his way to bigger things and can't afford this kind of scandal. At the moment he's doing God's work in Kansas City, seeking the very first of our ancestors."

According to Mormon scripture, the Garden of Eden was located somewhere in that Missouri town.

Traveler swung around in his chair and stared at the temple across the street. Beyond the walled temple grounds stood the Mormons' Genealogy Library, said to house just about every written record available on earth. "When it comes to investigations," he said, "you have everything at your fingertips already. An army of Danites if need be."

"Don't believe everything you hear about me," Ellsworth said.

"Are you saying you aren't the White Prophet?"

"What I'm saying, Mr. Traveler, is that I'm offering you a great deal of money, carte blanche if necessary, to do a job for me, which I can't do for myself. I want you to go down there and put this man under a microscope. Confirmation, that's what I want, on every rumor and every fact. I want you to act for me, to be my eyewitness on the spot. Naturally I want my grandson cured, but if that's not possible, I don't want him tormented by some cult country quack."

It had been late September the last time Traveler had been in cult country. He'd gotten to a place called Cow Fork, looking for a young runaway called Lynn Ann. Once again he could almost feel the furnace blasts of heat that had rolled over the blistered landscape as the small town shimmered in a late summer death grip. The heat and the thirsty soil had soaked up all that blood in the blink of an eye. The ground was red on red and the blood hardly showed.

Traveler shivered at the memory and turned his back on Salt Lake's prime temple view. "You must have people of your own who are better qualified."

Ellsworth folded his arms tightly across his chest. "I want a nonbeliever like yourself. If my grandson dies because of Thurgood . . ." He left the threat unsaid. Coming from the reputed head of the Danites, it brought the hair up on the back of Traveler's neck.

"A grandfather should know better than to put personal vanity ahead of his grandson's well-being," Traveler said.

Ellsworth took hold of his bag, fingered the ball of tar through the clear plastic, and shook his head slowly. "Chewing gum and candy, that's what seven-year-olds should think about, not Hodgkin's disease."

Sighing, he put away the bag, retrieved a snapshot from another pocket, and slid the photo across the desk. In it, a tow-headed boy was holding a puppy in his arms and smiling into the camera lens.

"That was taken last year," Ellsworth said. "He was six. This was taken last month."

A second snapshot showed a bald-headed, skeletal child propped on pillows. The impact on Traveler was visceral and sudden, not unlike a blind-side tackle from his old football playing days. He couldn't help comparing the boy's dispirited expression with that of the bright-eyed little girl that he and Martin had rescued from Bingham Canyon a few months back. No doubt the White Prophet had counted on Traveler making such a comparison.

"I'll need my father's help," Traveler said. "He's in Nevada at the moment, visiting an old friend."

"So I hear. A missing person, isn't it, your father's specialty as I understand it."

"It's more of a condolence visit."

"They tell me your father's in Pioche, just across the border. It would be an easy drive from there to Fire Creek."

Next to the photograph Ellsworth laid a credit card with Traveler's name on it, along with the name of the Church of Jesus Christ of Latter-day Saints.

Traveler stared. The card proved that the apostle's visit

wasn't the result of a spur-of-the-moment glance at the Chester Building.

Traveler was about to voice his suspicions when Ellsworth said, "I wouldn't delay if I were you. Young Josiah doesn't look like he can last much longer."

TWO

Traveler watched from his office window as Josiah Ellsworth's Tongans marched out into the middle of South Temple Street and held up traffic like school crossing guards. Only then did the apostle cross the sticky asphalt and disappear into the temple grounds.

A few cars honked, no doubt driven by Gentiles, the term applied to all non-Mormons. When traffic resumed, the tires made slapping, rainstorm sounds on the liquefying tar. Another ten degrees and South Temple really would turn into chewing gum.

A sudden yearning for a stick of Blackjack overwhelmed him. He rooted in Martin's desk, hoping for something to chew. All he found was an open, dusty-looking roll of Tums. He popped one in his mouth and sucked on it. It made him more thirsty than ever.

Five minutes of running the tap produced nothing but lukewarm water. Chester water, Martin called it, drinkable enough in the lobby but heating up as it rose through the Chester Building's ancient pipes to their office on the third floor.

Chester water was an August phenomenon, which Martin

blamed on Brigham Young. If he'd settled higher up the Wasatch Mountains, Martin claimed, instead of proclaiming his promised land in the middle of a desert sinkhole, his city wouldn't have to suffer through its yearly heat wave.

Traveler stepped to the east-facing window to check the Wasatch for himself. Their 10,000-foot peaks still showed the snow that provided the city with its year-round runoff, making the promised land possible.

Traveler mopped his face. Ellsworth was right. The office of Moroni Traveler and Son did need air conditioning. But the Chester Building predated such luxuries, and a window unit would spoil the view from either window.

The phone rang.

"What's the first rule of survival?" Martin said without preamble.

"Are you suggesting that I broke it?"

"A father knows when his son is getting himself into trouble."

Traveler checked the street again, half expecting to see his father on the sidewalk out front armed with a cellular phone.

Martin said, "Tell me that I'm wrong, that Willis Tanner's phone call was nothing but a bad dream."

"I should have known."

"You're damn right. That boy's been getting you into trouble since the sixth grade."

"What did he say?"

"It's what he didn't say that worries me. And how the hell did he know where I was? Pioche, Nevada, for Christ's sake. I'm having breakfast with my old friend Pete Biscari, the phone rings, and Willis says, 'Hi, Martin, I'm glad I caught you,' as if he'd just stepped across the street from the church office building to pay his regards. 'I have a message,' he says. 'From Moroni?' I ask. 'No,' he says, which gives me the willies, because I know he speaks for the prophet. So I'm sitting there, holding my breath, waiting for the word. And what does he say? 'If I were you,' he tells me, 'I'd stay there by the phone and wait for Mo to call.' Right then, I knew the church was involved, and that you'd broken my first rule of survival.''

"I haven't seen Willis in a week," Traveler said, blinking against the sweat running into his eyes.

"I don't have time to sit around here all day, waiting for you to call and confess.''

"Technically speaking, I'm not working for the church, so I haven't broken the rule.''

"Was Willis right? Were you going to call me?''

"Hold on a minute.'' Traveler set the phone aside, pulled his shirt over his head, and used a relatively dry spot to towel off his face. Considering the timing of Tanner's call, Josiah Ellsworth hadn't been acting on his own. At the very least, his request—the vetting of a potential messiah—had the tacit approval of the prophet.

Traveler tossed his shirt in the direction of the coat rack and picked up the receiver. "Since I'm going to need your help, I had to phone you sooner or later.''

"Let's hear it. Let's hear the shoe drop.''

"Josiah Ellsworth just left the office.''

Martin groaned. "I don't want to hear about it.''

"He wants us to look for the messiah.''

"I'm hanging up," Martin said, but there was no sign of a dial tone.

To himself, Traveler counted to fifteen before Martin said, "What did he really want?''

Traveler told him about Ellsworth's estranged daughter, a dying grandson, and a would-be messiah, all to be found in cult country, where polygamists and self-proclaimed prophets had been killing one another in the name of God for a hundred years.

"Do you remember what you said the last time you did business in cult country?''

"Remind me.''

" 'Never again, no matter who's involved.' Your exact words."

They both knew that was a misquote, that Traveler had said never again when a young woman and polygamists were involved. Particularly a young woman like Lynn Ann, whose name by tacit consent they'd never mentioned again.

Traveler said, "The subject of Kary came up."

"And what did he say about your mother?"

"Mostly he avoided the question, the same way you do."

"I know how he feels," Martin said, "because I can't go running off to someplace like Fire Creek. Pete Biscari's in bad shape. He needs a shoulder to lean on, maybe two. Besides, he'd like to see you again, Mo."

Biscari's son, Petey, had been missing for a little more than a month. Considering the desert terrain and 100-degree-plus temperatures in that area of Nevada, the official search had been called off a long time ago, as soon as survival was no longer considered possible.

"Is he asking us to investigate?" Traveler said.

"We'll talk about that when you get here."

"We're needed in Fire Creek."

"Young Petey went missing with another boy, whose body was found almost immediately. You'd understand why if you saw the terrain. A Gila monster would have a tough time surviving around here."

"Ellsworth's grandson, Josiah Smoot, is still alive," Traveler said quietly.

"The Ellsworths and the Smoots," Martin said. "Names to be reckoned with, church names that violate rule number one."

"You haven't seen the boy's picture. He looks like something from a death camp."

"They say Orson Smoot is a rising star in the church, maybe even a member of The Fifty."

■────────■

"No you don't. The White Prophet is bogeyman enough, without bringing in The Fifty."

They both knew that the names of The Fifty were a closely guarded secret. They were the men who controlled, anonymously, the finances of the Mormon Church, the wealthiest church in the United States.

Martin said, "The word on the street is that by marrying into the Ellsworth family, Smoot put himself on the fast track to becoming an apostle one day. Maybe even prophet. Not the kind of man you'd want for an enemy. And remember, Mo, this isn't one we're going to win. Sooner or later, Hodgkin's disease is going to kill that boy, and when it does some of the blame is going to rub off."

"I already told Ellsworth yes."

Martin snorted. "Men like Ellsworth usually get what they want, one way or another."

Traveler took a deep breath. "Ellsworth did admit one thing about Kary. He said he knew her. He came right out with it, as if he expected me to know that already."

"Your mother knew a lot of people, all of them her best and dearest friends until the next batch came along."

"What kind of male friends are we talking about?"

"I raised you most of the time, because your mother declined the responsibility. She never forgave me for that. I can hear her now. 'Look what you've done to that boy,' she'd say. 'You've influenced him to the point where he'll never make anything of himself. Another keyhole snooper is the last thing we need in this family.' "

Martin chuckled. " 'What will my friends think?' " he went on in a falsetto. " 'Every time I look in the Yellow Pages, I'll see Moroni Traveler and Son and know people are laughing at me. You might as well take away my temple recommend, and my chance at salvation.' "

"Kary didn't have a temple recommend," Traveler said, referring to the Mormon state of grace—all tithes paid, the Word of Wisdom followed to the letter—that allowed members in good standing access to the temple.

"I asked her about that once. 'It pays to have friends in high places,' she told me. 'A bishop here, an apostle there.' "

"Men like Josiah Ellsworth?"

"Like I said, her friends came and went."

Traveler remembered some of them, big men, as tall as Ellsworth, at least to a boy stranded among giants. Their names eluded him. *Angel,* Kary had called them, or sometimes, *my Moroni.* Their faces were lost in time, all except Marv's.

He'll be your new father, Kary had said when she left Martin and took Traveler with her to live in an apartment in Sugar House. *You'll change your name as soon as Marv and I are married.*

You'd better practice writing your new name now, Marv had told him, writing out a sample at the top of a lined page, the first in a thick notebook. *I'll be back later to check on you.*

Marv had laid a hand on the young boy's shoulder, squeezing just enough to transmit the threat. The remembered pain had kept him writing for hours, his head down, his face wet with tears, while Marv took Kary into the bedroom.

A week later Kary took her son with her when she went to see Martin about the divorce. *Marv's getting anxious,* she'd said. *He wants the settlement taken care of.*

How much does he want?

Half the house is mine.

Martin nodded. *What about our son?*

He'll be staying with me.

Martin had knelt beside his son. *Is that all right with you, Mo?*

Will I have to change my name like Marv says?

What?

He makes me practice writing it.

I'll talk to him. They'll be no more of that.

The next day, Kary and her son had moved back home. Her

stay was temporary, Traveler's permanent. He never saw Marv again.

"Answer the question," Traveler said. "Was Josiah Ellsworth a friend of Kary's?"

"Under the circumstances, I'd tell you if I knew with any certainty."

"Is there anything you can tell me?"

"Sure, I'll drive across the border and meet you in St. George. It's a hundred and five degrees here, so you'd better junk that Fairlane of yours and rent something that'll make it this far. You can drop it off in St. George."

Traveler sighed. "I should be there by dark."

"One more thing. Did you get a retainer from Ellsworth?"

"He gave me a church credit card with my name on it."

Martin laughed. "Now I know we're in trouble."

THREE

Traveler packed a bag for cult country: two .45 automatics, plus extra ammunition and a change of clothes. Martin already had his own overnight bag with him in Nevada, but no weapon.

For a moment, Traveler considered dialing Willis Tanner's private number at the Joseph Smith Memorial Office Building up the street, but had second thoughts. Knowing Tanner, nothing would be admitted, no White Prophet, no knowledge of a new messiah, and no advice worth taking. Not over the phone anyway. Tanner could only be pinned down face to face, if then. Even so, Traveler intended to give it a try.

He studied the face of the dying boy one more time before slipping the snapshot into his wallet, along with the church credit card. Then he locked the office and walked down the long hallway to the cagework elevator. One ring brought the exposed cables to life, humming in the windy shaft.

The elevator operator, Nephi Bates, opened the door with a smile.

"He stood where you are," Bates announced, "and gave me his blessing." He breathed deeply and deliberately as if proud to be inhaling the same air that the White Prophet had been occupying a few minutes earlier.

Traveler put a finger to his lips.

Bates nodded. "I understand. Mum's the word." He came to attention and stared straight ahead as he piloted them to the lobby, where Barney Chester was pacing back and forth, an unlit cigar clenched between his teeth.

"We need to talk," Chester said the moment the elevator door opened. He grabbed Traveler by the arm and led him across the lobby to the cigar stand.

"No you don't, Barney. My clients are confidential, especially when it comes to apostles."

"Who cares about you and your White Prophet." Chester thrust his mangled cigar into the eternal flame and lit up. "I don't believe in the Danites anyway. What I need is your help with Bill and Charlie."

"I'm on my way to rent a car."

Ignoring the comment, Chester slipped behind the counter and poured coffee into heavy white mugs that had been set out in advance. The counter was actually a glass-topped display case filled with pouches of Bull Durham, Chiclets chewing gum, and Sen-Sen. The display hadn't changed in all the years Traveler had been hanging around the Chester Building, first as a boy visiting his father's office and then as a tenant. The postcard racks were the same too, displaying scenes that had long since disappeared—the Sugar House penitentiary, the Coconut Grove, and Black Rock Beach. The cigar stand itself was sandwiched between two massive Doric columns of marble that gave the impression that they alone held up the vaulted ceiling with its WPA mural of Brigham Young leading his pioneer flock to the promised land of Zion.

"Artificial sweetener?" Chester asked, holding up the brandy bottle he kept hidden behind copies of the *Deseret News,* the church newspaper.

Traveler shook his head.

With a shrug, Chester topped off his own cup, took a long sip, and sighed. "You're the only one Bill and Charlie listen to. Back me on this one, will you?"

On cue, the door to the men's room opened and out came Bill, stepping sideways to clear his sandwich board from the jamb. Today's hand-printed proclamation read BAPTISMS PERFORMED. SEE BILL THE BAPTIST AT THE CHESTER BUILDING. Charlie was right behind him.

"You see what I mean?" Chester said. "With advertisements like that, I'm going to lose what tenants I have left."

The Chester Building, though an Art Deco landmark dating from the early thirties, couldn't compete with the air-conditioned concrete and aluminum structures that were turning Salt Lake into a California clone. As a result, only the long-time tenants remained, their offices emptying permanently as they died off. The present vacancy rate, Traveler figured, was about fifty percent.

Bill, known as Mad Bill, Salt Lake's Sandwich Prophet, so called because of the boards he wore over a long flowing robe, brought today's *Deseret News* out from under his front panel and held it up. A black, bold headline read WASHINGTON AND LINCOLN RAISED. Smaller type, about an inch high, clarified: NEW SAINTS ADDED TO CHURCH ROLLS.

"Soon there won't be anybody left," Bill said.

Charlie, Bill's Navajo disciple in their two-man church, raised a clenched fist. "Who's to say Geronimo and Sitting Bull aren't in danger?"

Mormon belief required that all properly documented deceased ancestors be raised to heaven through temple baptisms. Even Holocaust victims were being raised by Jewish converts.

"If we don't step in," Bill said, "everyone will be a Mormon

19

sooner or later. We must have our own baptismal font, right here in our temple.''

"I think they raised Thomas Jefferson last year," Traveler said.

Chester groaned. "Don't encourage them, Moroni. You got me into this last winter when it was so cold, by urging me to let them live in the basement next to the furnace.''

"You provided the bedding," Traveler said.

"They've declared my building a shrine.''

Bill stabbed a forefinger into the air, pointing at the recently restored ceiling fresco, where Joseph Smith's face, once hidden by generations of cigar smoke, had been revealed in the billowing thunderheads that rose above Brigham Young's wagon train. "We must raise our own army of the dead.''

Chester rolled his eyes.

"Come with me," Bill said, grabbing Chester by one arm while Charlie took the other. Together, they led him across the lobby to the plate glass window that looked out on South Temple Street. Traveler followed.

"There." Bill made a teepee of his boards, then ducked out from under them to point at a busload of young high-school-age males unloading in front of the temple gate across the street. "I know a field trip to heaven when I see one. It's probably time for a shift change, one relay team swapped for another. I can see them now, lining up in front of that great golden font, jumping in one after the other to steal souls before Charlie and I can get our hands on them. Thousands of souls every day, snatched away from us.''

"Maybe it's just a temple tour," Traveler said, though he knew Bill's assessment was probably correct. Raisings were said to run into the millions each year.

Bill said, "We must compete, Moroni. Give us our own font and Charlie and I will take turns dunking ourselves.''

Traveler winked at Chester. "It would keep them clean at least.''

Chester jerked free of Charlie's grasp. "For Christ's sake. I can't have them doing something like that. The church will picket me." He turned to eye the lobby as if assessing its potential for soul raising. "Besides, baptismals run into big money, not to mention the plumbing that goes with them."

Charlie raised a hand for attention. "It doesn't have to be elaborate. We could use a galvanized tub."

Bill hugged himself. "The water's heated in the temple."

Charlie stroked the peyote bag that hung from his neck. "God has provided us with insulation."

"You're not dragging a tub in here," Chester said. "This floor is genuine temple granite."

"We could run a hose from the men's room," Bill said. "That wouldn't cost much and that way we'd have hot water. What do you think, Barney?"

"I give up." Chester marched back to the cigar stand to relight his cigar.

Bill laid a hand on Traveler's arm. "What about you, Mo? How about a donation to help us raise souls from their fiery torment?"

"I've got a car to rent and work to do in Fire Creek. Until I get back, all I can spare is a little eating money."

With that, Traveler pushed through the ornate bronze revolving door and out into the scorching heat. Crowd noise caught his attention immediately. Up the block, where Main ran into South Temple Street, the landmark statue of Brigham Young was being hoisted onto the back of a flatbed truck.

Behind Traveler, the revolving door whooshed into action.

"It's a sign," Bill muttered as he and Charlie joined Traveler on the sidewalk. "History is being revised. Like Stalin and Lenin before him, Brigham is being demystified."

Brigham had been standing there in bronze since 1897.

"They're moving him out of the way, that's all," Traveler said. "He's been holding up traffic for years."

Bill shook his head. "We must spread the word, Charlie."

21

The Indian nodded. "Perhaps they're melting him down for commemorative coins."

"Or maybe he's hollow," Bill went on. "Full of incriminating documents and love letters to his twenty-seven wives."

With that, they rushed to join the crowd surrounding the displaced prophet.

Traveler left before trouble started.

FOUR

Willis Tanner agreed to meet Traveler in the lobby of the Joseph Smith Building, once the Hotel Utah. The lobby still had soaring marble columns worthy of a Greek temple. The walls were covered with elaborately carved gold scrollwork beehives, and the stained-glass ceiling put most cathedrals to shame. But the desk clerks, bellboys, and wealthy guests had been replaced by funereal docents, matrons mostly, one of whom sat at a desk facing an enormous alabaster statue of Joseph Smith. At Traveler's entrance, she smiled, gestured at the statue, and said, "We encourage our guests to touch the prophet."

Traveler was leaning against the alabaster statue when Tanner appeared ten minutes later. Tanner's squint, which appeared during times of stress, had narrowed one eye to a slit. His arrival sent the docent scurrying out of earshot. She, like everyone else in town, knew that he spoke for the church's living prophet, Elton Woolley.

"Mo," Tanner said in a hushed voice, "what brings you here?"

"Josiah Ellsworth."

The errant eye twitched.

"I want to know the ground rules before I go looking for the messiah," Traveler added.

"This is holy ground you're standing on," Tanner said. "And leaning on."

Traveler removed his hand from the prophet. "Let's start with Jason Thurgood. What's the official line on him?"

"The name means nothing to me." As he spoke, Tanner's eye closed down altogether. Such a reaction had been as good as a lie detector when they were growing up together, though now Traveler felt too many church-inspired nuances stood in the way to make it a totally accurate test.

"All right, Willis, tell me this. How many messiahs do we have in southern Utah at the moment?"

"Would-be messiahs, you mean."

Traveler shrugged.

Tanner rubbed his eye. "A week ago I would have said four. But a few days ago we had a shootout between a couple of brothers, both claiming the honor. One's dead and the other got himself pretty badly wounded. So that leaves us with two standing, which is about normal for that part of the state."

"Their names might help."

"Eli Nicholson down around Colorado City and John Elkins somewhere in the vicinity of Kanab."

Traveler nodded, relieved. Both locations were miles from Fire Creek.

"What about Moroni's Children?" he said.

"The last I heard they weren't claiming to have a messiah among them."

"Knowing you, Willis, the last you heard was probably ten minutes ago. Just tell me who I'm working for. You, Ellsworth, or the prophet?"

Tanner smiled lopsidedly. "You know what they say about cult country, Moroni. Never turn your back on anybody, even your wives.''

"That's not good enough, Willis. I'll walk away from this rather than go into that part of the state blind.''

"Let's take a walk,'' Tanner said, leading the way out onto South Temple Street. He headed north, toward the Lion House where Brigham Young had stabled his wives. Out front, Tanner paused to stare up at the ten gables that were said to represent the women's individual apartments.

"He had twenty-seven wives.'' Traveler shuffled his feet on the scorching sidewalk. "Not ten.''

Tanner smiled and replied, "It wasn't exactly a secret, Mo. Now what do you want to know?''

"Let's start with Moroni's Children.''

Tanner looked up and down the sidewalk, empty because of the 100-degree heat. "Some of this is only hearsay, you understand. Nothing has been proved against them other than trespassing, and those charges were never brought to court.'' He ducked his head. "Of course, that was in Arizona and by the time the authorities got involved, the Children had fled across the border to Utah.''

"Get to the hearsay, Willis.''

"The word is that they tried to take over a small town in Arizona, a place called Box Elder. There was violence. People went missing, or so the story goes.''

"Hold it. If people are missing, someone must be looking for them.''

"Box Elder isn't much more than a general store and gas station, just enough to service the surrounding ranches. There's no law to speak of, except maybe for the Highway Patrol which has better things to do than worry about back roads. There's no proof and probably no truth in the story anyway. People pull up stakes all the time and wander off in search of greener pastures.''

Traveler grabbed Tanner's arm. "We're not talking another Great Disappearance, are we?''

"Damn it, Mo. Keep your voice down."

"Look around you, Willis. No one else is crazy enough to be out in this kind of heat."

Shaking his head, Tanner led Traveler into the shade of a sycamore two houses away. There, Tanner pretended to admire the Beehive House, Brigham Young's personal residence, which his wives took turns visiting. Tanner's twitching eye made Traveler long for a polygraph.

"The Great Disappearance is a myth, Moroni. You know that. It never happened. It's just another urban myth."

"There's nothing urban about cult country."

"It was the 1930s, for God's sake, the Depression," Tanner said. "People moved around looking for work. So who knows what happened to a few malcontents."

Traveler had first heard the story from his grandfather, Ned Payson, who claimed the jawbone he kept on display in his dentist's office came from one of the dead. He'd finger it each time he got Traveler in the chair. Pretending to drill the yellowed fossil teeth, he'd say, "Mo, boy, I pulled this baby out of one of the skulls myself." He'd blow on his fingers as if savoring the memory. "It was all the evidence I dared take from the site. More than a hundred skeletons there were, too, bleaching in the desert sun. That was all that remained of those polygamists who bolted the church and headed south to start their own religion. Only they didn't move fast enough. The Danites caught up with them down near Kanab, just this side of the state line. The avenging angels killed every damn one of them, just like the Mountain Meadow Massacre."

Later, after Traveler had heard other versions of the Great Disappearance, all of which stressed the fact that an entire community had disappeared without trace, he asked Ned why he hadn't reported his skeletal find to the police.

Ned's answer had been to tap the side of his grandson's nose and say, "You never know who's a Danite, no matter what kind of uniform they're wearing."

Traveler tapped the side of Tanner's nose the same way. "Tell me, Willis, what's your instinct when it comes to Moroni's Children?"

"They're no longer welcome in Arizona, that's for sure."

"Forget Arizona. Tell me what I'm up against in Fire Creek."

Tanner took a deep breath. "Watch your back, Mo. That's always a good idea. We've got a disappearance there too. The mayor, I'm told. The word is he ran for reelection against one of the Children and lost more than votes. Though I'm betting it's just another urban myth."

"Is anybody looking for him?"

"Officially, he left town to go on a sightseeing trip."

"You're squinting again, Willis."

Tanner knuckled his wayward eye.

"If I disappear," Traveler said, "will you come looking for me?"

"I'll raise hell," Tanner said, wide-eyed for the first time.

"Give me some names, Willis, people I'm going up against."

"Moroni's Children are led by a man named Snelgrove."

"Are you sure he's not calling himself a messiah?" Traveler asked.

Tanner shook his head. "He claims he'll know the messiah when he sees him, though."

"Keep going."

"There's some guy who thinks he's the reincarnation of Orrin Porter Rockwell, old Brigham's avenging angel."

"Do you believe in reincarnation?"

"Only in heaven."

"You must have spies in the area," Traveler said.

Tanner spread his hands. "Okay, Mo, so we sent in a couple of missionaries. They were picked at random with no special training. We didn't want them to stand out. They were told to go about their regular duties. 'Ask no questions,' we told them. 'Don't draw attention to yourselves.' "

Tanner shook his head. " 'One question,' they told us later. 'That's all we asked, and they were on us.' "

"Who was?" Traveler asked.

"A mob of women. Apparently they surrounded the two and scared the hell out of them. You know nineteen-year-olds. They may be horny, but women still intimidate them, especially in bunches. Anyway, these two got run right out of town. Got damn near tarred and feathered to hear them tell it."

Tanner laughed. "Moroni's Children can't be so tough if they let a bunch of women do the fighting for them."

Traveler thought that over for a moment. "Let's get back to Jason Thurgood, then. What have you got on him?"

"I don't think he's the messiah, if that's what you mean."

"Ellsworth told me he was licensed to practice medicine in Utah. What else is there?"

Tanner shrugged. "We've been running computer checks, Mo. All we've come up with is the fact that he worked for the government at one time, but whatever he did for them is classified and unavailable to us."

"You can do better than that."

Tanner held up his right hand. "Scout's honor," he said, squinting badly.

FIVE

Two hundred and fifty miles later, driving a rental whose weekly rate was twice the value of his Ford Fairlane, Traveler reached the beginning of red rock country on Interstate 15. Cedar City was behind him, St. George ahead.

The highway passed between fortresslike sandstone pinnacles, whose bases had eroded into a blood-red soil. Mushroom-shaped clouds hung in the sky, their intermittent shade failing to dispel the heat. Their presence reminded Traveler that this was "downwind" country, downwind from Nevada's atomic test sites where people had been dying of radiation poisoning since the 1950s. Even the wildlife—the marmots, the porcupines, and the mountain lions—were gone. The politicians blamed their extinction on the coming of the interstate. The locals knew better.

Traveler groaned out loud. The locals had damn near gotten him killed the last time he'd been in this part of the state. It was barren country, beautiful only to tourists, and downwind from a lot more than fallout. Here, if the radiation didn't kill you, the apostates fleeing the church authorities in Salt Lake might.

Traveler stopped on the shoulder of the highway and checked his map. Cow Fork was forty miles due east.

He pulled back onto the road and the thump of his tires on the washboard surface seemed to drum out *Lynn Ann, Lynn Ann.* It was supposed to have been a routine pickup. Lynn Ann was underage, fifteen, from a good Mormon family, and probably already regretting the fact that she'd picked cult country as the site of her teenage rebellion.

Traveler hadn't missed the girl by more than a hour at the bus station in Salt Lake, though her destination had surprised him.

"You could have knocked me over," the window clerk told him, "when she asked for a ticket to cult country. Cow Fork, my foot. They ought to call it Polygamist City and be done with it, if you ask me. So I told her, 'The best I can do, is a dropoff on Highway 89.' 'That's all right,' she says. 'They promised to send a truck for me.' " The clerk shook his head. "A young girl like her. Them polygamists will be on her like hounds on a leg."

"I'm only half a day behind her," Traveler had said. "They won't have time."

"It's later than that, if I'm any judge."

Traveler hadn't caught the innuendo until he saw Lynn Ann for himself. By then he was surrounded by cult members, one of whom claimed to be the father of her child, which, judging by the size of her belly, was well on the way. Her father, Traveler's client, had failed to mention the pregnancy, only that his daughter was kicking up her heels.

"She's underage," Traveler told them.

"Not in God's eyes," one of them answered.

Traveler assessed the odds and decided to back off.

At his first step, Lynn Ann said, "If we let him go, he'll bring back help."

It was fight or run, he decided, scooping her up and making a dash for the car. The bullet went right through him and into her stomach.

That had been the last time Traveler had entered cult country unarmed.

By the time Traveler reached St. George, three hundred miles south of Salt Lake, the sun was setting. Martin's Jeep, already parked in front of the car rental agency, was covered with a layer of red dust. The windshield wipers had been used recently, leaving crimson streaks in the wake of their blades.

Martin was brushing dust from his jeans as he stepped from the office. "Come on, Mo. Turn in that car and let's get going. We've got an all-night drive ahead of us."

"It can't be more than a hundred miles to Pioche."

"Who said anything about Pioche? Old Pete has moved his sheep camp south of town and into the desert. The only way to get there is a dirt road. More of a track, really. Five miles an hour in the dark, he told me. And there's thirty miles of that ahead of us after we leave the Pioche turnoff."

Traveler had been no more than ten when he first met Petain Biscari, a Basque sheepherder working the foothills east of Salt Lake. In those days, he'd lived in a horse-drawn caravan, smelling of sweat and sheepdogs. Now, Biscari had an oversize four-by-four pickup truck with a full rifle rack and a camper shell attached. It was parked at the base of a scrub-covered rise where a small band of sheep was grazing in a tight bunch watched over by a black and white border collie. The surrounding desert looked too sparse to support much of anything, let alone sheep.

A second black and white border collie, its muzzle grayed with age, stood at Biscari's side. Traveler's boyhood memory of Biscari was of a tall old man. He still looked old, his weather-beaten face and neck like cracked leather. Only now he was half Traveler's size, short and wiry, with dark fierce eyes that denied his short stature.

When Traveler reached out to shake hands, hair rose along the dog's back.

"Easy, Janie," Biscari said. "These are friends."

The dog made a rumbling sound deep in her throat.

"She's like me," Biscari said. "She's getting old, too old to run sheep all day. That's why I keep her with me. Besides, ever since Petey went missing, she's sensed my mood and won't leave my side."

Smiling grimly, he led the way to an open fire and poured coffee into three metal mugs already set out, along with a can of Eagle Brand milk, as thick as honey.

When everyone was served, Biscari squatted on his heels, Janie beside him, and blew on his coffee. After a while, he said, "What have you told him, Martin?"

"It doesn't matter. I want to hear it again myself. We both do."

Biscari nodded but didn't respond immediately, concentrating on his coffee instead. He was a recent widower, Traveler knew from Martin's briefing during the night-long drive, a Basque who'd come to America to earn enough money to send back to the old country for the woman he intended to marry. They'd had one late-life son, Petain Jr.

Rather than squat, Traveler sat cross-legged on the ground, while Martin found a rock to perch on.

"When it comes to children, I'm lost," Biscari said, rubbing the dog's ears. "All I know is sheep. I've been moving them around in this desert for years."

He pointed east, toward a line of low hills along the horizon. "Over there's Utah. It's open range, and that's where I'm headed. It's the direction Petey boy would have gone, too."

Traveler started to ask why, then caught Martin's signal to let the man continue on his own.

"Our house is on the eastern edge of my ranch. For years I've been telling Petey, 'If you ever get lost on our ranch, east is home. Remember, son, if you don't know where you are, walk east.' Only this time, it wasn't home he wandered away from. Walking east would have meant suicide."

With an angry gesture, Biscari threw the dregs of his coffee into the fire. The hiss caused Janie's ears to flatten against her head.

"Petey's sixteen but . . ." Biscari began. He tapped the empty mug against the side of his head. "He's still an eight-year-old up here. As long as his mother was alive, she took care of him. But I'm not getting any younger, and he has to learn to get by on his own. At least, that's what I thought. Maybe I was being selfish, I don't know. But I couldn't run a sheep ranch with Petey under foot. That's why I sent him to that damned clinic. We'd been talking about it before Miriam died. When she knew she didn't have much time left, she sewed his name in his underwear so he wouldn't lose them. She'd skin me alive now, for losing Petey."

Shaking his head, he pulled off his faded red neckerchief and mopped his face with it. "The Echo Canyon Clinic, it's called, over near Pioche and less than an hour's drive from my place. Close enough for me to see Petey every weekend, I figured, and I did, too. But I didn't listen, not when he told me he didn't like the place. I guess I thought he was upset because he'd never been away from home before. Besides, what could I do? I don't have any close relatives in this country, nobody to see to him after I'm gone. And they promised me at the clinic that they'd teach him a skill. His doctor, a man named Ottinger, seemed very nice."

Biscari tied his neckerchief back in place.

"It's a government clinic specializing in treating the retarded,"

Martin said for Traveler's benefit. "They told Pete their program makes boys like Petey self-sufficient."

"It doesn't matter what they told me," Biscari said. "I'm to blame. I promised my Miriam I'd take care of Petey." His shoulders sagged. "Then a month ago, they said Petey ran away with another boy named Tad Whitlock—the ringleader they called him. I met Tad on one of my visits. He was even . . . more simple than Petey. How could he have been a ringleader?"

He rose to his feet and circled the fire, his hands thrust against the small of his back, the dog at his side. "I'm no fool. Petey's been missing a month now. A full-grown man can't last much more than a day in this country, not without proper provisions."

"What about you and your sheep?" Traveler asked.

"I know the water holes. Otherwise I wouldn't risk it."

"You should have called me sooner," Martin said.

Biscari winced. "The sheriff told me he'd have them back before the sun set. When that didn't happen, I knew it was already too late. What I want now is to find what's left of the boy and bury him. If I don't, Miriam will never forgive me. That's why I'm moving the sheep. Chances are I can't find him out there, but I've got to try. All my life I've gone with the sheep. Now they come with me."

"What can we do?" Traveler asked.

"Find out why he ran off."

Even without a reason, Traveler felt certain the clinic was legally responsible. Martin must have been thinking the same thing, because he said, "You might be better off hiring yourself a lawyer."

"Martin," Biscari said softly, "we go back a long time, since the day you kept me out of jail. I couldn't pay you back then, you wouldn't have taken it. I can pay now, though, whatever you and your son ask."

"We'll talk to them at the clinic," Martin said. "No charge."

Traveler groaned at the thought of the government red tape ahead.

"I won't take charity," Biscari said.

"Then we'll settle for one of those jackrabbit stews of yours," Martin said. "Where can we get in touch with you?"

"I'll keep heading east, like I said. I'll water near the Echo Canyon reservoir, then cross over into Utah somewhere north of Uvada. There's good water near there, not that I think Petey could have made it that far. From there . . ." He shrugged. "I'll keep going east until I run out of range."

"That ought to be somewhere near Fire Creek, shouldn't it?"

Biscari shook his head. "I don't think I'll get that far, not in this kind of weather."

SIX

The Echo Canyon Clinic was ten miles northeast of Pioche, Nevada, in a bleak stretch of desert. To get there, Traveler and Martin swung off Highway 93 just beyond what looked like a small government housing project, and onto a two-lane black-topped road that showed no numerical designation of its own. From there to the clinic, they didn't pass so much as an outhouse. The last five hundred yards had a posted speed limit of five miles an hour, enforced by six-inch speed bumps.

Two ten-foot chain-link fences, one inside the other, provided a security perimeter for the clinic's main building, a two-story cinder-block square the size of a Kmart.

"The fences are new, Petain told me," Martin said, "since the boys ran off."

Traveler negotiated the last bump before coming to a halt next to a guardhouse the size of a tollbooth. The man who emerged wore a tan uniform and a pistol belt. A radiation badge hung from his shirt pocket.

"We called ahead," Traveler told him.

Five minutes later they were given badges of their own and escorted into the office of the clinic's administrator, Dr. Harold Grant, who was on the phone.

"I'll be right with you," he mouthed, waving them into a pair of leather chairs that faced his desk.

His office was large by government standards, and appointed with thick wall-to-wall carpeting and a large cherrywood desk whose highly polished surface contained half a dozen framed photographs, all angled to be visible only to his visitors. The faces in the photos looked happy and carefree from a distance. Up close, the features of Down syndrome were apparent.

Grant's gray suit coat hung next to the door with a radiation badge clipped to the lapel. Another badge hung from his shirt pocket.

Into the phone he said, "It's not funny, Emerson. I'm tired of you people in research thinking you can get away with murder. Your specimens are to go straight to the laboratory and never be delivered here. Repeat, never, no matter how big a laugh you think it is."

He paused for a moment, listening. "No you don't. I heard what you did to my predecessor. An animal lover, wasn't he, a bleeding heart for every one of your pretended mistakes that mysteriously showed up in his office. Well, you missed the mark with me. I don't care how fuzzy they are, I'm not getting attached. As for your latest delivery, he can sit here until he starves for all I care."

Grant swiveled his chair to stare at something in the corner of his office, beyond Traveler's line of sight. "He's been here since yesterday. And no, I'm not feeding him, and I'm not naming him either."

He faced forward again, listening and getting red in the face. "I don't give a damn if your area *is* secure and off limits. In one hour, I'm sending my secretary to dump him outside your door."

Grant rolled his eyes for Traveler's benefit. "If she can't get past the check point, I'll do it myself."

Traveler tilted his chair far enough to see a wire mesh cat carrier sitting on a pile of newspapers in the corner of the office. The cat inside, a calico with badly matted fur, lay curled in a ball, breathing heavily and watching Traveler with frightened eyes. There was no sign of a water bowl or food. RADIATION PROTOCOL was stamped on the side of the carrier in red letters.

"If that doesn't work, Emerson, I'll dump him in the desert myself. And don't start talking about cruelty to animals, not after what you people do to them in that lab of yours."

Martin stood up to take a look at the cat for himself.

"I'm starting the clock now," Grant said. "You have one hour." .

He hung up and shook his head apologetically. "You'd think scientists would have better things to do than behave like children. If it weren't for bottom-liners like myself, this place would fall apart, I swear."

A pitiful meow punctuated his remark.

He swung around and gingerly kicked the cat carrier. "You see what I have to put up with all day."

Traveler forced a smile. "Exactly what are they doing to the animals in that lab you were talking about?"

Grant spread his hands. "I don't like it either. But we're talking cancer research here. If a few animals have to die to save human lives, well . . ." He shrugged.

"I don't understand," Martin said. "What does animal research have to do with retarded children?"

"That's government funding for you. They have this facility out here in the middle of nowhere and they don't like to waste it. So they set aside one wing for mental health. Of course, we do a lot more than research here. We also treat cancer patients."

Martin leaned forward, shaking his head. "How do you treat children like Petey Biscari?"

Grant picked up a manila folder, the only item of business on his desk. "I see by my records that Petain Biscari is the sole relative listed, so what is your interest?"

"We're friends," Martin said.

"Professional investigators," Traveler added, "like I told your secretary on the phone."

Grant shrugged. "The authorities tell me that survival in our desert around here is an impossibility after such a long time."

"Mr. Biscari needs to bury his son," Martin said.

"He refused our offer of crisis counseling."

"Tell me," Traveler said. "How many patients Petey's age do you have here?"

"This may sound unbelievable, but I don't know. We do government work at this facility, you understand, and much of what goes on is classified. Even as clinic administrator, I'm not allowed full access, as you could hear on the phone."

"Why would the treatment of mentally disabled children be classified?"

"Research is expensive, Mr. Traveler. The companies producing some of our experimental drugs want to protect their investment."

"Hold it," Martin said. "Mr. Biscari told me his son was being retrained to take care of himself. Drugs were never mentioned."

Grant shook his head impatiently. "Our retraining program is done in conjunction with drug therapy. It's clearly outlined to all our parents when they enroll their children with us. They have to sign a waiver." He opened the folder, removed the top document from a half-inch stack, and pushed it across the desk toward Martin. Passages had been highlighted in yellow in advance.

"What kind of drugs were being used on Petey?"

"I wouldn't know, and I couldn't tell you if I did. That's the rules. Everything's in our disclosure statement. I tell each and every parent who comes in my office, read everything carefully.

Most of them don't, I'm afraid. Obviously, you two haven't read it either.''

Traveler forced a smile. ''Are we talking radiation therapy?''

''I couldn't say.''

''Why the radiation badges, then?

''You must understand,'' Grant said. ''Children like Petey are a terrible burden on their parents. They never grow up, really. Everything has to be done for them. In public they can be embarrassing. So it's perfectly understandable that parents should feel a sense of relief when they turn responsibility for these youngsters over to us. A great many of them don't even come back to visit, sad as that may seem.''

''Petain Biscari trusted you,'' Martin said.

''I don't know him personally, of course. But as I said, we did offer counseling. Eventually, there may be some kind of compensation forthcoming, though it's not my place to make that kind of commitment. Certainly, we've taken elaborate precautions since the two boys wandered off.''

''You mean the fences?''

Grant nodded. ''Your client should take comfort from that.''

''That's not good enough,'' Traveler said. ''Petey told his father he didn't like it here at the clinic. We want to know why.''

''He got the best of care, I can assure you of that.''

''We'd like to see that for ourselves.''

''Only immediate relatives are allowed that privilege.''

''Then how about an interview with the boy's doctor?''

''A Dr. Ottinger,'' Martin added.

''I'm sorry. He's left us. Talking to anyone else is out of the question.''

Grant rose, walked to the door, and opened it. ''We don't give out personnel information.''

Traveler looked around him. Everything, Grant included, was anonymous government issue. No doubt that was necessary when dealing with laboratory animals, human or not. There was no way to win against such people or their bureaucracy. But Traveler still had to do something. One life, he decided, would be better than nothing. He moved around the desk and picked up the cat carrier. "Did the calico sign a consent form?"

"Don't force me to call security."

Traveler crossed the room and poked a finger against Grant's chest. "There's no winning against people like you. God knows what you're doing to the children in here. I'd take them out of here if I could."

"That cat's government property," Grant said.

Traveler smiled. "You don't want to see me again, but you will if you try to stop me saving at least one life in this damn place. It's not much, I grant you. But it's better than doing nothing at all."

Grant stepped around Traveler and picked up the phone on his desk.

"I wouldn't do that," Martin told him. "When my son gets mad, I can't control him. You can see how big he is. You wouldn't believe the damage he could do before help arrives."

Grant cradled the phone. "You'll never get past the gate."

Martin shook his head. "If I were you, I wouldn't call after we're gone. You see, we find people for a living, no matter where they hide." He smiled. "Have a nice day."

SEVEN

Traveler held his breath all the way to the car, expecting alarm bells to go off at any moment. At the gate, the guard didn't even look up from his magazine as he waved them through.

"I'll be damned," Martin said when they were back on the highway. "We got away with the bluff."

"I wasn't bluffing," Traveler said.

Martin squinted at him, then at the cat carrier in the back seat. The calico, more wild-eyed than ever, was emptying his bladder.

"Switch the air conditioner to maximum and drive like hell," Martin said. "Our friend back there needs water and something to eat. Dogs and cats can't sweat like we do, so this kind of heat can kill them fast."

When they reached the highway and turned toward town, Traveler said, "What the hell was going through Biscari's mind, leaving a kid in a place like that?"

"Whatever it was, it can't compare with what's going through his head now."

As soon as they reached Pioche, they negotiated all-day parking in the service bay at a Texaco station, plus cat-carrier space in the air-conditioned office. The mechanic on duty also threw in information free of charge, confirmation of what Traveler already suspected, that most of the married workers from the clinic lived in the government housing outside both Pioche's city limit and its legal jurisdiction.

Traveler raided a news rack, stocking up on newspaper to line the carrier. After that, he and Martin bought two Styrofoam ice chests at a grocery store, one for cat food, water, and soft drinks, the other filled to the brim with ice bags for emergency cooling in case the Jeep's air conditioner died on the way to Fire Creek. They also picked up a plastic box and a bag of kitty litter.

Once everything was stowed in the office next to the cat, who had gone through two saucers of water and half a can of food, Martin sat down to study the local phone book.

"There's a veterinarian listed," he said. "What do you think? Should we take Brigham for a checkup?"

"How do you know his name's Brigham?"

"Because he's got more lives than Brigham Young had wives."

Traveler shook his head. "He looks perky enough to me."

"Let's find ourselves a beauty parlor, then." Martin went back to the phone book. "Here we go. Marcia's Salon Elegant. When we get there, I'll do the talking. You look far too threatening."

Ten minutes inside the beauty parlor got Martin an invitation to dinner from a local widow, and the name Janet Ottinger, with an address in the government housing project.

Ms. Ottinger, as she insisted on being called, had that tanned, sinewy intensity of someone obsessed with physical fitness. Her white tennis outfit, shorts and revealing pullover, showed the results of years of hard work.

When they told her they were detectives looking for her husband, she smiled like a lottery winner and invited them inside.

"As of next month," she announced as soon as they were seated in her air-conditioned living room, "thanks to the divorce laws here in Nevada, Ms. Ottinger will disappear forever. That's when I say 'I do,' and become Mrs. Sheppard. After that, the name Ottinger will never be mentioned again, not by me anyway."

Traveler nodded sympathetically. Bitter divorces were an investigator's best friend, with only the slightest prompting needed to start the venom flowing.

"Where can we find your ex-husband?" Martin said. "We want to talk to him about one of his patients at the clinic."

"He's gone crazy," she said. "He ran off, away from me, a perfectly good job, and a good salary."

She looked around the austerely furnished room, whose only extravagance was an enormous television set. "This may not be the greatest place to live but the rent is practically nothing. In another year, two at the most, we would have had enough money saved up to move to California. But no, Jack couldn't wait. He up and disappeared."

"Why?" Martin asked gently.

She wet her lips. "Like I said, he went crazy. One day he comes home from the clinic and says, 'I've been hearing voices.' 'What kind?' I said, thinking it was the beginning of some kind of joke. You know what he said then? 'It's my conscience I'm hearing.' "

She paused to tuck her legs under her. "As soon as I heard that, I knew he'd lost one of his patients, probably one of the younger ones. Every time that happened, he got depressed. I always did the best I could to help. I took him to bed, if you know what I mean, but talk was all he wanted. 'Two boys,' he said. 'I can't face the parents. I can't lie anymore.' "

"What did he mean by that?" Traveler said.

"Your guess is as good as mine." She hugged herself. "If you ask me, being dead is better than being retarded like those people. I told Jack the same thing that night he was going on about that damned conscience of his. I thought he was going to hit me when I said it. The next thing I knew, the bastard walked out and never came back.''

"Do you know where he went?

She shrugged. "I didn't give a damn.''

"What can you tell us about the clinic?'' Martin asked.

"When we came here, we had to sign all sorts of documents, swearing to keep quiet. I could go to jail if I said anything.''

"What about your future husband, does he work there?''

"Another doctor? Forget it. They think they're gods. Mark has his own TV repair business. These days that's as good as being a doctor or a plumber.''

She nodded at her large-screen set. "I met him when he made a house call. Thank God, I won't be paying his repair prices anymore.''

"Is there anyone else in town we can talk to about the clinic?'' Martin said.

"I've told you all I can.'' She unfolded her legs, smiling at Traveler's admiration of them. "Mark thinks he's lucky to get me, and he's right.''

She walked them outside into the blazing desert sunlight. Halfway to the curb, she stopped to say, "Jack told me never to say anything I'd be sorry for inside the house. He thought the security people from the clinic had hidden microphones in the walls. I wouldn't put it past them to spy on what people got up to in their bedrooms, though with Jack and me that wasn't much for a long time. Anyway, you talk to John and Clea Whitlock. They moved to Pioche to be near their son while he was being treated at the clinic. He and another boy ran away and died in the desert. Just don't tell anyone you got their names from me.''

"We understand they do radiation research at the clinic,'' Martin said.

"It's no use asking me about it,'' she said. "All I know is everybody who goes anywhere near the clinic has to wear a radiation badge. As I understand it, the place got its start right after World War Two. Something to do with the atomic bomb program. Only then it was just a bunch of wooden barracks and Quonset huts.''

"Did you ever visit your husband's place of work?" Traveler asked.

"Only once. I hate to say it, but I feel uneasy around retarded people.''

"Was your husband's work helping them, do you think?"

She shrugged. "Maybe that's why Jack didn't want children, because of the risk of something going wrong. Maybe they zapped his balls with all that radiation. I don't know. But it must have been dangerous. He always showered out there at the clinic and then again when he got home, until all the hot water ran out too, the inconsiderate bastard.''

EIGHT

The Whitlocks' house, a faded 1950s green stucco square, sat on an unpainted cinder-block foundation surrounded by white gravel. The only vegetation visible was two potted cacti resting on a concrete slab outside the front door. A FOR SALE sign hung from a metal post next to the rural mailbox.

The Whitlocks stood side by side behind their screen door and examined Traveler's card. They looked to be in their early fifties, the same age as their house and just as dispirited.

"When we saw you park out front," Mrs. Whitlock said, "we hoped they'd sent you over from the real estate office."

"We're here about your son," Traveler said.

She stepped back, edging behind her husband, who read Traveler's card again.

"Are you working for the government?" Whitlock asked.

"Petain Biscari," Martin said. "We're helping him with his son."

Whitlock latched the screen door. "He's gone too, just like our boy."

"Can you tell us how it happened?"

"We were told not to talk to anyone."

"Mr. Biscari needs your help," Martin said.

The woman sighed. "He should accept the fact that his boy's dead. Still, I know how he feels, so ask your questions."

"Start by telling us about your son."

She leaned against her husband. "Our Tad used to talk about Petey Biscari. They were friends. They . . . we don't know why . . . but they went off together."

"Mother, I can't take this," Whitlock said. "Besides, you know what they told us. Speak to no one." He backed away from the screen, turned, and disappeared through an open doorway leading deeper into the house.

For a moment Traveler thought the woman was going to shut the door in their faces. Then she unlatched the screen and beckoned them inside.

"I'm sorry there's no place to sit," she said, "but we shipped our furniture back home, when the clinic said they'd buy our house if it didn't sell by the end of the month."

"It feels good to be out of the sun," Martin said.

"I'd ask you into the kitchen for a cold drink, but my husband isn't up to company yet."

Martin nodded. Traveler said, "Do you have any idea why your son ran away from the clinic?"

She shook her head.

"Was your son receiving any kind of radiation therapy?" Traveler asked.

"That part of the clinic was strictly separate. They promised us that, because we didn't want our boy mixed in with patients who might be sick or dying."

"A boy doesn't run away unless he's unhappy," Martin said.

"We said the same thing to his doctor when he came here."

"Dr. Ottinger?"

"That's right. He and another man. Dr. Ottinger said we were his first stop and that he was going on to the Biscari place.''

"The last time Biscari saw him, Petey was still alive,'' Martin said.

She tried to smile but her lips didn't have it in them. "If it hadn't been for the doctor, they wouldn't be buying our house, you know. He said someone had to pay. He made the other man put it in writing. They had a big fight after they left, because I could see them yelling at each other in the car.''

"Who was the other man?''

"The man who runs the clinic, I think. He gave my husband his card, but I don't remember the name.''

"Could you ask your husband?''

She shook her head. "John's afraid of getting stuck here in the desert with this house. Maybe he's right. Maybe they'll renege if they find out I've been talking to you. He has to get away. We both do. It's our only chance of escape.''

"From what?'' Traveler asked.

She looked away, unable to meet his eyes. "From something neither of us dares admit. From that moment when we heard the news that our Tad was gone and the burden of him was lifted.''

49

NINE

Traveler and Martin drove back to the Texaco station, picked up Brigham and their ice chests and headed for Fire Creek, intending to avoid the heat by driving at night. Neither spoke for miles. There was no need. They both knew there was nothing more they could do for Pete Biscari short of a full-scale background investigation, which could take weeks. The Smoot boy, in the final stages of Hodgkin's disease, took precedent.

According to the map, the road to Fire Creek should have been paved. But when Traveler and Martin reached the turnoff no asphalt showed in the high beams from the Jeep's headlights, only crushed rock and red dirt.

Traveler braked to a stop while Martin checked the map again. Ahead lay the great Escalante Desert, colored a stark white on the map and overlaid with a red-lettered warning in the legend: CARRY DRINKING WATER ON THESE ROADS.

"We passed a gas station a while back," Martin said. "Let's

pick up more water." He leaned over the seat and spoke to Brigham. "What do you say, cat? How many lives have you got left?"

Sighing, Traveler reversed the Jeep onto the shoulder and drove back the way they'd come, to Wagstaff's Highway Haven, one of those stucco relics from the thirties.

The moment Traveler pulled in beside the old-fashioned glass-topped gas pump, the station's screen door banged open and a man came out to greet him. He wore one-piece, grease-stained overalls, had gray unkempt hair and a week's worth of whiskers. He could have been forty-five or sixty.

He grinned and said, "I saw you pass by a few minutes ago, son. At night, in this kind of weather, the smart ones double back. Do you want a room or a fill-up?"

Traveler eyed a rusting metal sign. LAST CHANCE GAS, WATER AND LODGINGS. NEXT STOP 70 MILES.

"I'll start with some water," he said.

The man smacked his lips, a sound of approval. "There was a time when water bags were made of canvas and hung on every bumper in these parts. Now there aren't any real bumpers, and all I've got is plastic jugs. How many do you want?"

"That depends on the road to Fire Creek."

The man ran a hand along the fender of the Jeep Cherokee. "I wouldn't take a decent car on what's left of that road, son. I know they call these things sport utilities, and they show 'em on TV climbing mountains, but out in that desert . . ." He shook his head. "I'm Silas Wagstaff, by the way, and I don't travel anywhere around here without at least half a dozen gallons of water with me. If you're smart, you'll stay over in one of my cabins out back for the night."

"How long's the drive to Fire Creek?" Martin asked.

"Maybe three hours in daylight."

"And in the dark?" Traveler said.

"There are more things out there to worry about than potholes and rock slides. Most of them walking on two feet, if you get my meaning. But suit yourself, Mr . . ."

"Moroni Traveler and son."

Wagstaff snorted. "Named you after Joe Smith's angel, did they. His Moroni brought God's word on golden tablets. What do you have to say for yourself?"

"If you're going to rent us a room," Martin said, "you'll have to settle for plastic."

"There's three of us," Traveler added. "We've got a cat in the backseat."

Wagstaff shrugged. "What do you say to twenty bucks a night, and I'll throw in coffee in the morning, unless you're following the Word of Wisdom."

"Coffee's fine."

"This will be a first for me, serving caffeine to a Moroni. Hell, I'll throw in some bacon and eggs and milk for the cat. Come on in and I'll take your plastic and get you a key."

The gas station office couldn't have been more than ten feet square. Cases of motor oil, replacement parts, cartons of bottled water, and a stack of tires lined the back wall. A small counter the size of a card table stood in the middle of the room; it held an antique brass cash register. The metal folding chair behind the counter had a Coors logo on its back. A metal rack full of dusty Twinkies, cupcakes, and candy bars stood next to the door. A Coke machine old enough to have THE PAUSE THAT REFRESHES printed on the side took up what space remained.

Traveler handed Wagstaff the church credit card provided by Josiah Ellsworth. Without looking at it, Wagstaff edged behind the counter, opened the cash register, took a key from one of the coin drawers, and handed it to Traveler. "Yours is the second cabin in line. I live in the first one. There's no TV unless you want to watch with me."

Traveler nodded at the Coors sign. "We could go for a cold beer."

"If you don't mind waiting a few minutes till I close up, I'll join you. I keep them in with the Cokes, but the Highway Patrol drops by sometimes this time of night, and I wouldn't want them catching me selling and drinking it on the premises."

"Do they patrol Fire Creek?" Traveler asked.

"Now and then, but Fire Creek's not much of a town these days. I have a kid sister living there, though why she stays I'll never know. Ruth Holcomb. She's a widow just about your age."

He looked at Traveler expectantly. When Traveler didn't respond, Wagstaff continued. "I've been asking her to leave Fire Creek for years. We have family ties here, she keeps telling me. Me, I lit out on my own right after high school. Back then Fire Creek still had some life. Now . . ." He shrugged. "Our parents are buried there. Ruth's husband too. She says somebody has to tend their graves, but it's a waste of time, if you ask me. We've got too many graves around here, what with towns dying out and turning into ghosts. 'So get away,' I tell her. 'Get married again.' "

Wagstaff raised an eyebrow at Traveler. "You're not keeping up your end of the conversation. Are you married, or not?"

"He needs a wife," Martin answered.

"Are you going to be staying in Fire Creek?"

Traveler nodded.

"Two strangers showing up at the same time is rare in this part of the country, which makes me wonder if you're not government men."

Traveler hesitated to tell the truth. The last thing he wanted was Wagstaff calling the news ahead to his sister.

Glaring, Wagstaff moved around the counter to rap a knuckle against a faded newspaper article taped to the front window. "You see this? It's the apology we got back in 1990. It took Congress nearly forty years to get around to it, saying they're sorry for killing us with their fallout. A little late, don't you think? Half my friends are gone, called home by cancer and leukemia. Good Mormons most of them, so you can't blame smoking for what happened to their lungs. My wife's gone, God rest her, just like Ruth's husband. Do you know how they got it, their cancers? I'll tell you. From drinking milk, for Christ's sake. From cows grazing on contaminated range, with the government lying through its teeth and looking the other way.''

Wagstaff stepped out the door and stood staring up at the night sky. The temperature had dropped enough to make Traveler roll down his sleeves. Martin did the same.

"Take a deep breath, son, and tell me what you smell.''

"Pine trees and sage,'' Traveler said, "and something that reminds me of buckwheat.''

"I smell Harry. 'Dirty Harry,' we call him. That's the bomb they set off in 1953. The wind was blowing this way and they knew it. There were thunderheads in the sky waiting to pick up the debris. They knew that too. But they had a delegation of congressmen waiting to see the sky light up, so they let her blow. They turned St. George into Fallout City. That's what the newspaper called it. To this day, they say Geiger counters still go off the scale out around Fire Creek. So you can see why we don't like government men around here.''

"We're not from the government,'' Martin said.

"It's not just the radiation you have to worry about. It's Moroni's Children. No kin, I hope.'' Wagstaff grinned at his own joke.

"Tell me about them,'' Traveler said.

"I have to do business around here, you don't. I don't ask about a man's religion when he's spending money. I will say this. Fire Creek was all but a ghost town, what with the old-timers dying off and the young people moving to the big cities. Then the Children arrived and gave it new life. Even the Indians had stopped coming into town from the old Shivwits reservation. They're dying off, too, I guess.''

Wagstaff went back inside to process Traveler's credit card. He ran it through the machine, printing out a receipt before bothering to look at the name and expiration date. "For Christ's sake. It says Church of Jesus Christ of Latter-day Saints.''

Traveler nodded.

"Are you sure you'll be drinking beer?''

Before Traveler could answer, a siren whooped in the distance.

"Here comes the Highway Patrol, on time as usual,'' Wagstaff said.

As soon as the car passed by without stopping, Wagstaff opened the Coke machine, took out three beers, and passed them around. After a long drink, he said, "The last strangers to take on Fire Creek were a couple of missionaries Salt Lake sent in. The pair of them got run out of town.''

"Is that your way of asking our business?'' Martin said.

"Technically, it's none of mine. But I know one thing for sure. Fire Creek doesn't attract tourists. For starters, the road is a son-of-a-bitch. Chunks of it disappear every time we have a gully-washer. Only last week I tore out a muffler trying to get around a slide.''

"Are there any strangers in Fire Creek at the moment?'' Traveler asked.

"I knew it,'' Wagstaff said. "As soon as I saw you I said to myself, 'Silas, here's trouble. You're here about the woman and the little boy.' Am I right?''

"We'd rather not say,'' Martin said.

"You can't keep secrets in a small town, not for long anyway. Word always gets out. The word I hear is that she's related to some high church mucky-muck. What do you say to that?''

Traveler shrugged.

Wagstaff said, "Someone named Moroni might get his ass in a sling considering the way things are in Fire Creek these days. I hope you know enough to be careful of Moroni's Children.''

"They're polygamous, we know that much.''

"That doesn't cover it. There used to be half a dozen cults within a hundred miles of here. They were scattered up in the White Hills, in the Castle Cliff area of the Beaver Dam Mountains, in places nobody else wanted. They had one thing in common. They all said that they alone knew God's will, that their way was the way of the true messiah and that all others were agents of the devil. For years they've been killing one another in the name of God, but never in great numbers. Then along came Moroni's Children, settling in the Furnace Mountains around Fire Creek, and suddenly they're the only cult left in these parts. So what happened, you might be asking yourself. Did the others see the folly of their way and convert?''

He stopped speaking to finish his beer. "You know what the good folks around here think, don't you? That Moroni's Children killed off the competition. That the desert's littered with unmarked graves.''

Wagstaff sighed. "They say you can see the old Mormon Trail from our satellites two hundred miles up. They say the wagon wheel tracks are still there, etched in the grass of the Great Plains after a century and a half. So why the hell can't they find some recently dug graves? I'll tell you why. You'd need an army to find anything in that desert. Even then, you couldn't cover everything. It's too goddamn rough, too hot, and too dangerous. So what I'm saying is, if the heat and the snakes don't get you, the polygamists will. Judging from the look on your face, you know that as well as I do. Besides which, you don't look like the kind of men seeking religious enlightenment. So why the hell are you here?''

He raised a restraining hand. "Don't bother lying, let me guess. Let's start with the woman and the child. Is she related to an apostle or not, or is that just gossip?''

Traveler wasn't about to invoke the name of Josiah Ellsworth if he didn't have to. "I've heard a lot about a man named Jason Thurgood. People tell me he works miracles."

Wagstaff chuckled. "I wouldn't know about that, but my sister might. She strings for one of the papers up in Salt Lake, and's been thinking about writing an article on his good works."

"Who's the law in Fire Creek?"

"They're too small to have anything but a town marshal. Edgar Peake's his name, a good man, but don't expect him to go up against the Children. Still, you ought to be safe enough as long as you stay out of the desert. Even the Children don't like calling attention to themselves if they don't have to."

Wagstaff tilted his head as if trying to see Traveler from another angle. "Looking at you, they might make an exception. So take my advice and check in with Ed Peake as soon as you hit town. When he's not marshaling, he's pumping gas or hanging around city hall."

TEN

Sunrise the next morning was like turning on a gas burner. The nighttime cool evaporated in an instant. Heat waves sprang from the red soil. The smell of sage and pine was quickly erased by the creosote stink of softening asphalt.

Traveler and Martin, already awake and dressed, were surprised to find Silas Wagstaff waiting for them by the Jeep. Six plastic jugs of water, a bag of ice, and a grocery sack stood alongside the car. Two coffee mugs and a shallow bowl were sitting on the hood.

"I promised you breakfast," Wagstaff said.

"We thought we'd get an early start," Martin told him.

"That what's I figured when I heard you moving around in the dark this morning. I packed you bacon sandwiches and threw in some Twinkies. There's canned cream in the coffee and you can take the mugs with you if you want. The cat bowl, too. I'll keep an eye out for you, and when I see you've made it back from Fire Creek, you can return the china. If you don't show, I can always run another charge on that fancy credit card of yours.''

He squinted at the bright, cloudless sky. "Take my advice. When you leave the blacktop, keep your speed to ten miles an hour, no more. That way you'll reach Fire Creek in three, three and a half hours. Any faster and you'll blow a tire for sure. Or maybe worse. If you get stuck out there, don't wander off. Stay with your car. Never more than a day or two passes before somebody comes by.''

Wagstaff shook their hands. "Don't forget my sister, Ruth Holcomb. If you have to stay over, she'll put you up." He winked. "If you get up to anything with her, you'll have to answer to me.''

From Highway 18, the road to Fire Creek rose steadily toward the northwest. Exactly as Wagstaff had said, ten miles an hour was the optimum speed. Any faster and the washboard surface threatened to shake the Jeep to pieces.

The landscape grew more desolate with each passing mile. Only bayonet-leaved yuccas grew close to the road. Farther out, clinging to the sides of narrow gullies, drought-stunted piñon pines looked on the verge of spontaneous combustion.

After a two-hour steady climb, they reached the crest of a low range of hills that didn't show on the map. Traveler slowed the Jeep to a stop and found himself looking down into a sinkhole that stretched for miles before butting up against the blood-colored Furnace Mountains in the distance. A mirage lake shimmered along their base.

He squinted against the glare but saw no sign of Fire Creek. According to the map, the town stood at the base of those mountains, though why anyone would settle in such a place was beyond his imagination. Surely Brigham Young's declaration that southern Utah would become his Dixie, his land of cotton to clothe the faithful, couldn't have included the Escalante Desert.

Martin leaned over from the passenger seat to check the gauges. All were within the normal range.

"Let's hope the air conditioner holds out," he said. "Brigham looks like he's run out of lives."

Traveler opened one of the plastic jugs and swallowed a mouthful of tepid water while wishing for a beer. After Martin took a swig, they began the descent into Fire Valley. Even at ten miles an hour, the four-wheel drive raised a red dust cloud that trailed behind them like a smoke signal.

By the time they reached the ragged asphalt that delineated Fire Creek's Main Street an hour and a half later, their hair, their clothes, the car's upholstery, the entire surface of the vehicle were covered with a clinging layer of red dust. Their lips were caked with it. Traveler's mouth felt gritty. Brigham had changed from calico to ginger.

City hall stood at the head of Main Street fifty feet from where the blacktop started. It was a squat, one-story building, fronted with rough-cut red limestone. Two narrow, jail-like windows were set into the rock on either side of a weathered door. The wooden sign over the doorway, black and cracked with age, had carved lettering: FIRE CREEK CITY HALL, 1870. DOWNWIND had been spray-painted over it in Day-Glo red.

No one was on the street, though half a dozen vehicles were scattered along the three blocks of asphalt before Main Street turned back into desert and disappeared into the nearby foothills. The squat one-story buildings closest to city hall, the Goldstrike Barber Shop and Perry's Dry Goods, were boarded up.

Grabbing the open water jug, Traveler climbed out of the Jeep and rinsed his hands. Martin did the same, before retrieving the cat carrier and carrying it into city hall, a single room with white-washed walls and a rough-planked floor showing a grooved path leading to a large desk. Behind it sat a man built like a sumo wrestler.

"Marshal Peake?" Traveler said.

Nodding, the man stood up. He was a foot shorter than Traveler's six-three, but every ounce his equal, two twenty at least. He wore no uniform, only jeans and a short-sleeve knit shirt that clung to his muscled chest. He carried no gun, though a shotgun and rifle were locked in a rack on the back wall.

Traveler and Martin showed their IDs.

Peake raised an eyebrow. "Seeing the two of you together, maybe I should call the county sheriff for reinforcements."

"Just think of us as summer tourists," Martin said.

Peake gave Martin the old one-eye. "Judging by the size of your partner, you've brought in too much firepower for anything as simple as a look-see."

Martin laid a hand on Traveler's shoulder. "Looking at him, I know it's hard to believe he's my son. I think my wife must have slipped him some extra hormones when he was a kid."

Peake circled Traveler once before moving back behind his desk. "I know you now," the marshal said. "I used to see you on TV, playing pro football. You looked bigger."

"I had to bulk up to survive," Traveler said.

Martin said, "I tried teaching him tennis, but he didn't have the coordination."

"You two can cut the bullshit." Peake clenched a fist, causing muscles to ripple in a forearm twice the size of Traveler's. "We don't have much around here worthy of a look-see, and I haven't seen a real tourist in years. So what we're talking about, one way or another, is Moroni's Children. And they don't like outsiders poking their noses in. Neither do I, because I have to clean up the mess when they start ganging up on people like you. Usually, it's sightseers who want to see polygamists, or maybe young bucks who want to join in the fun so they can have all the wives they want."

"That may be the only good reason I can think of for living in a place like this," Traveler said.

"You'd have to be born here to understand why we stay. I tried

61

your big city and didn't like it." He leaned back in his chair and laced his hands behind his neck. "If it's not Moroni's Children you're after, it must be the shooting."

"Shooting's a criminal matter," Martin said. "Nothing to do with us."

Peake rocked forward and stood up. "It's the Smoot woman, then. The word is she's related to one of the apostles. And don't bother looking surprised. This may be the sticks, but I know enough to check on new people who move into my town."

He stepped to the open door. "Look out there. You don't see people on the street, do you? That's because I warned them you were coming, and I wanted to get a first look at you."

"It's a hundred and five degrees out there," Martin said. "It's no wonder the streets are empty."

"I think Marshal Peake got a call from Silas Wagstaff," Traveler said.

"He was only being a good neighbor."

"He doesn't know our business and neither do you."

"Silas's not the kind of man to ignore someone like you. Neither am I. I phoned Salt Lake to check up on you. My brother officers don't exactly love you up there, but they don't have any black marks against your name either. They also say you don't come cheap, which makes me wonder who's paying the freight. Silas says you've got a church credit card. Is that right?"

Traveler eyed his father, who raised an eyebrow right back, a look that said Edgar Peake wasn't the kind of marshal he'd expected to find in a place like Fire Creek.

"Credit cards are a wonderful thing," Martin said.

Peake nodded. "If you're worried about the Smoot woman, she's perfectly safe. Not even the craziest of Moroni's Children—and there are some dandies—would risk the wrath of an LDS apostle."

"We're not here as bodyguards," Martin said. "Just observers."

Peake stared out at the empty street. "There are times when I wish I had a bodyguard myself."

Traveler said, "It would be a lot easier if you told us where you stand when it comes to Moroni's Children."

"Easier for you, maybe." Peake turned his back on Main Street. With the noontime glare behind him, his expression was impossible to read. "I'm only a part-time marshal, when I'm not pumping gas. Mine's the only station in town, by the way, open by appointment. Most people don't want to get on my bad side, in case I cut off their gas ration. Of course, what you really want to know is whether I'm a member or not. In this town, that's the right question to ask, that's for sure, since not much goes on around here that Moroni's Children don't have a hand in."

"That doesn't quite answer the question," Traveler said.

Peake snorted. "I left Utah for a while, right out of high school. It gives you perspective. You meet someone in Denver, say, or maybe Phoenix, you don't ask their religion. It's considered impolite. But here in Utah, that's the first question people ask. If you give the wrong answer, they don't want anything to do with you. So the only answer I'm giving is this. Everyone in town, the old-timers and the Children, too, got together with the council and decided they needed someone neutral to handle the drunks and what-have-you. Since I'm the strongest man in town I got the job. That's not a boast. I took on all comers in arm wrestling and put them down."

The marshal, staring at Traveler, added, "The way I see it, a show of strength is the best way to keep the peace."

"We'll do our best to keep it that way," Martin said.

Behind Traveler, someone knocked on the doorjamb. The woman standing there, silhouetted against the dazzling sunlight, was tall, maybe five-ten, with square shoulders and a straight waist.

"I'm Ruth Holcomb," she said.

As soon as Marshal Peake made the introductions, she crossed the room to shake Martin's hand first, then Traveler's.

"My brother told me to keep an eye out for you," she said. "He didn't say anything about an animal."

"He said you could put us up," Traveler said.

"There's just us and our cat," Martin added.

"You know what they say, three's a crowd." Her smile created deep wrinkles around her eyes and mouth. She was a widow, Silas Wagstaff had said, about Traveler's age. Somewhere in her early forties, Traveler guessed, smiling back at her. She was hefty without being fat, with closely cropped black hair, finger-combed by the looks of it, flecked with gray. Her jeans were the no-nonsense kind, with rolled-up cuffs and baggy knees. Instead of a blouse, she wore a loose man's shirt with the sleeves cut off at the shoulders, exposing deeply tanned, solid-looking arms. The hang of the shirt emphasized her substantial breasts.

"If Ruth can't put you up," Peake went on, "I don't know where you'll find another bed in town. She boarded our missionaries a while back, until they wore out their welcome."

"The marshal makes it sound like I'm running a boarding house. We don't get tourists in Fire Creek, and not many visitors either, except a few sightseers looking for polygamists. Those, I don't take in. The truth is, my house is too big for a woman on her own, not that I can't use the extra money. I can provide meals too, if you want them."

"We have our own cat food," Martin said.

Peake snorted. "There's only one restaurant in town, the Escalante Cafe, half a block up the street."

Ruth shook her head. "You've been a bachelor too long, Ed, if you call that place a restaurant."

The marshal raised his hands in surrender. "You won't get any argument. Ruth here's the best cook in town."

"You never came back for seconds."

"We'll take a room," Martin said.

"I've got two spares if you want them."

"Missionary rooms, we've been calling them lately," Peake said, "though maybe now we'll have to rename them."

"You haven't asked how much," Ruth said.

Martin shrugged.

"Thirty-five dollars a day apiece, including meals."

"We'll take the two of them," Traveler said.

"I'll have them made up for you in an hour."

"We'd like to look around town for a while," Martin said. "Maybe we could drop off the cat now?"

"I'll take him for you," she said, reaching for the carrier. "Dinner's at six. I'm one block east and half a block north, the two-story brick house on the corner of Fillmore and First."

"First is Nephite Street now," Peake said.

"I don't care what the Children renamed it, it's still First to me."

"They have the votes on the council, Ruth. You know that."

"If I had my way they wouldn't be able to vote." She nodded at Traveler. "I hope you're here to cause trouble, like everybody's saying."

■   ■

ELEVEN

Marshal Peake insisted on treating Traveler and Martin to lunch at the Escalante Cafe. As soon as they walked in, Traveler knew the reason why. Nearly a dozen men were there ahead of them, scattered among half as many tables. Each table was covered in oilcloth, faced by four bentwood chairs, the teacher's models Traveler remembered from grade school. None of the men was eating, only staring at the new arrivals, sizing them up and, if Traveler read their expectant eyes correctly, awaiting the marshal's next move.

The cafe occupied the lobby of what had once been the Escalante Hotel. The front desk had been reclaimed as a lunch counter with chrome and Naugahyde stools attached. Country music, muted by a swinging porthole door, came from the kitchen. The room's pine plank floor had been painted brown to match the metal embossed ceiling. A sheet of bare plywood had been nailed over the stairway leading to the second floor.

"Quite a crowd for a town this size," Martin observed.

"Just the regulars," Peake answered. "Old-timers and friends who grew up with me."

Traveler studied the faces. If there were any members of Moroni's Children among them, they showed less zeal than Mad Bill, and far fewer trappings. No beards, no robes, no placard prophecies, only middle-aged wear and tear.

The marshal stepped behind the counter to tap a fingernail against a Coca-Cola thermometer on the back wall. "Ninety-five. It was 96 in here yesterday and 110 outside on Main Street."

He led the way to an empty table that stood in the center of the room. Grinning, he sat down and nodded for Traveler and Martin to do the same.

Traveler clenched his teeth, knowing that he and Martin were being put on display.

"There's no need to order," Peake said. "Annie only serves one dish. Today's Saturday, so it's meat loaf. She'll bring it out of the kitchen once we give her the word we're ready."

Martin nudged Traveler under the table to show he knew what was going on. "I could eat now."

"No you don't," someone said.

"Not before we've had our fun," another added.

The comment drew ragged cheers from the onlookers.

"I'd introduce you to everybody," Peake said, "but that would be too many names to remember. There was a time when Mayor Gibbs would have been here to welcome you personally. He would have done the honors and then seated you right here, at his table."

"Rest his soul," someone intoned.

"Our new mayor's one of Moroni's Children," Peake said as he pushed up the sleeve of his knit shirt until the material bunched around his armpit. Then he lowered his elbow onto the oilcloth and smiled at Traveler. "It's best to get these things out of the way right up front, so we know where we stand."

"Arm wrestling proves nothing."

"Edgar's letting you off easy," one of the bystanders said. "Usually he knocks newcomers down and stomps on them. He says it softens them up."

Traveler waited for the laughter to subside before responding. "I let my father handle things like this."

Peake snorted derisively. "He's an old man."

Traveler mopped the sweat from his face to keep his smile from showing. Like so many others before him, Peake had failed to notice Martin's right arm, twice the size of his left, the result of a lifetime of tennis and strong-arming for beers.

"This here's Moroni Traveler," Peake goaded. "He used to be a linebacker for L.A. People said he played mean and crazy."

"You can't believe what you see on TV," someone answered.

The marshal spread his hands. "You see, Traveler. A reputation doesn't mean shit unless you're willing to prove it here and now."

"My reputation is long gone."

"There are some who might say you don't have the stomach to face a man one on one."

Traveler shrugged. "If you want me, you have to come through my father."

Martin rolled up his sleeve.

"Come on, Ed," someone shouted. "He looks pretty tough for an old bird."

"Maybe Edgar's gone soft," another said.

Peake stared at Martin and shook his head. "I'll go easy on you, old man. But your son had better watch himself when his turn comes."

Martin adjusted his chair until he and Peake were facing one another. When they locked hands, Peake's arm, seen side by side with Martin's, looked enormous.

Everyone in the cafe crowded around.

"Say when," Martin said.

"Take your best shot."

Peake's counterthrust levered Martin's arm a quarter of the way toward the tabletop. For a moment, Traveler thought the contest was over, that Martin's arm had passed the point of no return. Then he saw the grin fading from the marshal's face, and knew that his father was stringing it out.

Half a minute passed before Traveler coughed to catch Martin's eye, a signal to hurry things along. Martin immediately began applying pressure. Peake grunted as his arm was forced upward, past the starting position, and then down to defeat.

"Jesus," someone said, "nobody's ever beat Edgar before, young or old."

"It's a matter of leverage," Martin said.

"Bullshit," Peake responded. "You beat me fair and square."

"Maybe we'd better elect ourselves a new marshal," one of the bystanders said. "Someone older."

"I couldn't beat Martin either," Traveler said, coming to Peake's defense. "He's tricky."

Traveler tapped his father on the shoulder. As soon as Martin abandoned his chair, Traveler sat down and put his elbow on the table.

Peake's eyes had lost their fight. "I need a little time to get my strength back."

"I've seen you take on half a dozen, one after the other," someone catcalled.

Traveler put on a good show, prolonging the contest, but Peake won in the end. After that, the locals filed by, slapping the marshal on the back before returning to their tables. By then the marshal had caught enough breath to shout, "Hey, Annie, the show's over. You can serve lunch now."

A few moments later the kitchen's porthole door swung open and Annie appeared carrying a large tray stacked with plates. She served the marshal's table first. The meat loaf reminded Traveler of his mother's cooking, something from a can disguised to look homemade.

Without looking up from his plate, Peake whispered, "Thank you, Traveler."

"For what?"

"You let me win."

Traveler shrugged.

"It taught me a lesson, that's for sure. I owe you one."

"We'll settle for some information on Moroni's Children."

Peake filled his mouth with meat loaf and chewed thoughtfully for a while. "Until they came along, we were on our way to becoming a ghost town, like most every place else in this part of the state. Without them, there wouldn't be much left open in Fire Creek, maybe not even the Escalante.

"The Children bought a partnership in Shipler's General Store across the street. If they hadn't, Shipler's would have closed and the rest of us would be driving all the way to St. George for groceries."

"How many Children are we talking about?"

"All told, there's maybe a hundred and fifty, though some say the count's as high as two hundred. The elders have taken over some of the abandoned houses along Mormon Road. That's their name for it anyway, even though the signs still say Parowan Avenue. But the bulk of them are spread all over town in abandoned houses. A few have squatted in Coffee Pot Springs. That's a ghost town about a mile from here up in the foothills."

"How do they earn their money?" Martin asked.

"Some say donations. Others aren't so kind. I've heard stories of intimidation and blackmail, but nothing you could prove. Whatever they have, they sure don't spend it on material goods."

The marshal pushed his plate away. "Going by the number of pregnancies you see, there are a hell of a lot more of Moroni's Children on the way. Another generation or two and they'll control this whole damn county, just like they do this town."

"They must have registered to vote to elect themselves a mayor," Martin said.

"Only the men registered, twenty or so."

Martin raised an eyebrow.

"I know what you're thinking," Peake said. "I've done the math myself. It works out to about five wives per man, though some of the elders have more."

Traveler looked around the cafe. "How do the locals feel about Moroni's Children?"

"That depends on who you talk to. A couple of businesses are running in the black for the first time in years. Others have changed hands, though not without some hard feelings and maybe some laws broken. A couple of locals actually tried to join up, young bucks who got their underwear in an uproar thinking they could latch on to an extra wife or two."

"Did they?"

Peake shook his head. "Norm Kimball and Hank Woodruff started sniffing around the women as soon as the Children hit town. The next thing I knew, they disappeared. I alerted the sheriff and the highway patrol. I even spent some time out in the desert looking for their graves, but so far . . ." The marshal spread his hands in a helpless gesture.

"If you found the bodies," Traveler said, "who would you go looking for?"

The marshal pushed his chair back and stood up. "Let's see if we can walk off some of Annie's meat loaf."

The moment Traveler stepped outside, the heat sucked his breath away, but Peake seemed unaffected as he led the way across Main Street. Traveler and Martin followed, wading through heat waves and sticky asphalt, bypassing Shipler's for Benson's Funeral Home next door, a single-story clapboard that looked as if it hadn't been painted since the pioneers arrived.

Peake tugged a key-laden ring from his pocket and opened the door. "Desert burials put old Jessie Benson out of business, but we keep the electricity on because this is the only place with a working air conditioner."

71

As soon as they were inside, Peake switched on the window unit, which rattled ominously before settling down to a constant throb. Sighing, he stood in front of the vents and raised the front of his shirt to catch the stale-smelling breeze on his bare belly.

"I've known those men back at the Escalante all my life, but when it comes to Moroni's Children and murder suspects, it's best to keep your thoughts to yourself."

He squirmed, redirecting the air flow. "As for the Children, I'm not sure I trust any of them. I sure as hell don't feel comfortable around them. They feel the same about us townspeople, I guess, because they stick together like glue. They have their own kind of government. Horace Snelgrove's in charge, like a mayor or governor, and Orrin Porter handles law enforcement, though from what I hear all he has to do is glare and people get meek mighty damned quick. All the men vote on communal matters, the women do what they're told." He snorted. "You have to hand it to them for that. My wife told me to go to hell and walked out years ago."

Peake pivoted until the breeze was at his back. "I always figured I could take anybody when it came to a fight. A fair fight anyway. But I wouldn't tangle with Porter, not on your life. Just looking into his eyes gives me the creeps. I'm not the only one either. Everybody in this town walks on eggs around him."

Traveler started to say something but Peake beat him to it. "I know what you're thinking, that it can't be his real name. Orrin Porter Rockwell was Brigham Young's bodyguard, his avenging angel. So what, I say. This guy's just as mean, if you believe the stories."

"Do you?"

"If he thinks he's Rockwell's reincarnation, I'm not about to call him a liar. Don't either of you try it either, no matter how good you are at arm wrestling. The fact is, I got you out here alone to warn you off. I overheard one of the Children talking about you. I think maybe I was supposed to overhear, but that doesn't change the fact that you're on their enemies list."

He chuckled. "Yeah, they actually have one, a long parchment scroll maybe five feet long. They keep it rolled up in a leather case. Each name is written in red ink, I'm told, or maybe in blood, to hear some tell it. Anyway, your names are the latest additions. Porter did the honors himself, I hear."

"We're honored," Traveler said.

"Don't take it lightly," Peake said. "The name before yours was our missing mayor, Jake Gibbs. Nobody's seen him since. So my advice is to get back in your car and drive on out of here before the sun goes down."

Martin shook his head. "That's probably why they let you listen in. They wanted you to tell us that. You do the dirty work and their hands stay clean."

Peake shrugged. "If they added my name to that list of theirs, I don't know if I'd have the guts to stick around."

"I don't get it," Martin said. "Why have they made us an enemy?"

"Like I said, I overheard some of the women talking in Shipler's. They claim you're Danites, here to extract blood atonement on order of the church up in Salt Lake."

"That's crap," Martin said.

"I'm not saying I believe it," Peake said. "Maybe they don't either. But that's what I was meant to hear. That you're a Danite working for the White Apostle."

"There goes our cover," Traveler said.

Smiling, Peake held a hand in front of the air-conditioning vents. "What do you know. The air's damn near cold. Maybe hell's going to freeze over after all."

"Which reminds me," Martin said, "in case of heatstroke, I understand you have a doctor in town. Where do I find him?"

The marshal squinted so hard the skin around his eyes quivered. "I think I just heard a shoe drop, didn't I. Silas Wagstaff warned me to keep an ear out for it."

———————

He shaped his fingers into a gun and fired a mock shot at Martin and Traveler, one after the other. "If you want a second opinion on arm wrestling, I'm the man to come to. If you want a second opinion about a man like Jason Thurgood, you'll have to talk to his competition. Her name's Hanna Eccles. She's been nursing folks around here for as long as I can remember. Midwifing, too, at least until Thurgood showed up."

TWELVE

Hanna Eccles lived at the edge of town. Her backyard was nothing but desert, twenty miles of it, all the way north to the Bull Valley Mountains. Her ramshackle house, blackened clapboard nailed over partially exposed tarpaper, sat precariously on the lip of a deep, dry wash. A rough-cut sandstone retaining wall, built as protection against flash flooding, was sagging as badly as the disintegrating wooden steps that led to the front door.

Traveler tested the bottom step, which creaked but held his weight, then backed off to wipe the sweat out of his eyes. Martin, who looked none the worse for their walk in the 105-degree sun, was staring back the way they'd come, along Jaradite Avenue past Main and Pine Streets. Like most pioneer Mormon towns, Fire Creek had been laid out precisely, with streets running north and south and avenues east and west, a miniversion of Brigham Young's master plan for his City of Zion, Salt Lake.

" 'They who believe not in the Messiah shall be destroyed by fire,' " Martin said.

" 'For behold, the day cometh that shall burn as an oven,' "
Traveler responded.

"Your mother would be proud that you remembered your Sunday school," Martin said as he started up the steps.

The door opened before he could knock. The woman standing on the threshold was wearing a crisp white nurse's uniform, bright enough to make Traveler squint against its sun-sharpened glare. One look at her told him that she'd dressed expressly for their visit.

"Hanna Eccles?" Martin asked.

"Tell me they're right about you two," she said, nodding. "That you bring the wrath of God with you." Her gray hair was pulled back into a tight, precise bun; her gold-rimmed glasses sparkled. Her figure was trim, almost girlish, but her wrinkled face placed her somewhere in her sixties.

Martin handed her a card.

"Moroni Traveler and Son," she read. "Praise God. Jason Thurgood is about to get his."

Martin smiled. "I use the name Martin since my son came along. I had the cards printed up before I made the change, and it seemed a shame to waste them."

"We're not here in any official capacity," Traveler said. "But we would like to find out if it's true what they say about Thurgood, that he works miracles."

"They used to say that about me." Hanna beckoned them inside.

Her tiny living room had whitewashed pine walls, an oval multicolored rag rug covering most of the plank floor, a catalog sofa and two matching chairs wrapped in plastic slips, and an upright piano that was being used as a shelf for dozens of framed photographs.

When she saw Traveler looking at the photos, she said, "My patients used to give me likenesses of themselves as a testament of their cures."

Hanna carefully arranged her uniform skirt to keep her knees from showing, then sat down on the sofa. Traveler and Martin took the flanking chairs, whose plastic slipcovers crinkled under their weight. Between them was a glass-topped coffee table covered with precisely arranged magazines.

"Tell us about Jason Thurgood," Martin said.

"Did you notice the creekbed on your way in?" she responded.

They nodded.

"It's called Fire Creek like the town, though some around here have rechristened the place Downwind." She shook her head as if to deny the new designation. "Outsiders figure our town is named for the fiery color of the Furnace Mountains. The rest of us know better. It's named Fire Creek because its runoff quenches the heat whenever we get summer thunderstorms up in the Bull Valley Mountains. We used to be able to count on one or two gully-washers every August. But the last two years have been bone dry. Some of us think it's a punishment for going against the word of God by accepting Moroni's Children. If that's true, then I say Jason Thurgood is the last straw. I say he's an agent of the devil."

"Not everyone agrees with you," Martin said. "What would you say to those who call him a miracle worker?"

"I have better things to do with my time than listen to gossip."

"What about his failures, then?"

She wet her lips. "Judging by the way Moroni's Children have taken to him, I figure any mistakes are buried out in the desert somewhere. Out there, they're in good company at least."

"Do you have any proof that someone's been buried?" Traveler asked.

She shrugged again.

"We hear Mayor Gibbs is missing," Martin said.

"For a long time now, people have been leaving Fire Creek if they get the chance. So it's hard to keep track of who's pulled up stakes and gone off on their own without being forced. But Jake Gibbs was like me. Too set in his ways to change, or even to try.

So he's six feet under for sure. Otherwise, he'd been in town raising hell at what's going on."

"Let's get back to Jason Thurgood, then," Traveler said.

"I never made much money helping people, just enough to supplement my Social Security. But he and his fancy ways put an end to most of that."

"Is there anyone else in town who might be willing to talk to us about him?"

She smiled, adding wrinkles to her face that paradoxically made her look younger. "Why don't you come out with it and ask me for the names of his enemies, besides myself of course?"

"That would be helpful."

She waved for them to stay put, then got up from the sofa and moved to the piano, where she began running a finger over the tops of various framed photographs. Finally, she selected one and held it up. "You might want to talk with Ben Moffit. He left me for Thurgood for a while, but soon came back. You'd better hurry, though. Old Ben hasn't got much time left."

She replaced Moffit's photograph and chose another. "Karl Cederlof used to be an important man around here. The fact is, he owns most of the land Moroni's Children are squatting on, not that it's worth that much, you understand. Unless of course they hit another mother lode like the old days. Karl's a big city man these days, living up at the county seat in Parowan."

"That's Iron County," Martin said. "I thought we were in Washington County."

"There are places around here where it depends on which side of the road you're standing on, or maybe who you're talking to. Moroni's Children like to keep close to all the borders, state and county, in case they have to make a quick move to escape the law."

She stepped directly in front of Traveler and stared up at him. "I'm hoping that one look at you and Moroni's Children will move on and take Jason Thurgood with them."

"Exactly what is his relationship with them?" Traveler asked.

"It's a pact with the devil, if you ask me."

"Is he a member?"

"Not as far as I know. I'll give him that much credit. He uses them as volunteers, but only because they came to him and offered their help. If I'd offered first things might have been different."

"It almost sounds like you admire him," Martin said.

"I respect a doctor's kind of knowledge. If he can heal people by laying on hands, so much the better. But I keep asking myself, why would an educated man come to a place like this when he could be making big money up in Salt Lake? Look around you. You can see I don't have much to show for my life's work. The people I help pay the best way they can. Most times, it's nothing more than groceries, or maybe some plumbing work, or patchwork on the house."

She shook her head sharply. "There's no money to be made in Fire Creek."

Martin stood up. "Would you go to Jason Thurgood if you were sick?"

Hanna smiled. "It's hard to say what people will do when they're feeling bad enough."

THIRTEEN

Traveler and Martin followed Hanna's directions, walking south on Enterprise Street to where it intersected Brigham Avenue at the other end of town. Along the way, a few front yards showed a scattering of hand-watered shrubs. There were no lawns, no shade trees to speak of except for a ragged line of cottonwoods and desert willows growing along the bank of the dry creekbed. Judging by their limp foliage, another August without runoff might do them in permanently.

"That woman Hanna reminded me of your mother," Martin said as gusting wind, like exhaust from a furnace, began raising a haze of fine red dust. "Hard women, both of them. Your mother used to say, 'I want my son to be a doctor. Doctors don't go through hard times. Even the cheapest people will spend every dime they've got for a cure when death's staring them in the face.'"

"One Christmas Kary gave me one of those doctor sets with a toy stethoscope."

"She asked me to buy you a real one once, but I told her you were too young to take care of it. 'You'll have no one to blame but yourself,' she said, 'if my boy doesn't turn out to be a rich doctor.' 'In that case,' I told her, 'think of the good time you'll have reminding me of it.' "

Ben Moffit's house—more of a hammered-together shack built of mismatched pieces of lumber and scrounged metal signs advertising Hires Root Beer, Technocracy, and Sonora Phonographs—stood beyond the asphalt on the northwest corner of Brigham and Enterprise. Attached to one side was a narrow lean-to providing shade for a frail-looking man sitting in an aluminum deck chair.

"You'd be the detectives everyone's talking about," he said. He looked to be eighty at least, fleshless and completely bald. Despite the heat, he was wearing a heavy blue flannel shirt, buttoned all the way to the collar. "They say the Angel Moroni himself comes to call us home when the time comes."

His laugh rattled with phlegm. "Judging from the direction you came, I'd say Hanna sent you down to check up on me." He jerked a thumb over his shoulder. "There's some folding chairs against the back wall somewhere if you want to sit yourselves down."

Traveler fetched them, old card-table chairs rusting at the joints and wobbly when unfolded. He placed one on either side of Moffit.

Martin sat down and came right to the point. "Hanna tells us you left her for Jason Thurgood."

"That's what I figured," Moffit said, nodding. "The church sent you down here to put a stop to him."

Rather than trust his full weight to the chair, Traveler braced a foot on the dented metal seat. "Do you think he needs to be stopped?"

"It's mostly the stories going around about him that rile folks. Miracles and the like. But that wasn't the only reason I went to him. You see, I never did like being examined by a woman. It's embarrassing, if you know what I mean. Anyway, I took myself out into the desert to talk to this man Thurgood. He didn't charge me for the examination, I'll say that for him. He was friendly too, not like some of those so-called Moroni's Children who hang around him. He didn't beat around the bush either, just told me flat out there wasn't anything he could do for me. The cancer's got me like damn near everybody else around here.''

He reached down, grabbed a handful of dirt, and tossed it toward the front of the lean-to where the breeze caught it. "It's blowing in from Nevada today like always. Downwind from hell, that's Fire Creek. It's a wonder we all don't glow in the dark.''

"Tell us more about Jason Thurgood," Martin said.

"All things considered, I'd have to say he's a good man. He offered to make arrangements to have me sent to a hospital up in Salt Lake. He said they could give me a few more months with some kind of special treatments, but I told him to hell with that. So he said he'd do what he could to make me comfortable. You know what it means when doctors start using words like that. It's all over but the shouting. So I took his pain pills and went back to Hanna. I told her what she wanted to hear, that he was nothing but a charlatan. But I really went back because she doesn't have anybody else to talk to these days. 'Hanna,' I said, 'I'm yours for the duration.' Besides, my wife Erma, God bless her, has already gone on ahead. The sooner I catch up with her the better. My Erma was a saint, she was. One woman like that should be enough for any man, not like some around here who think they're Joe Smith come back to life.''

Moffit tilted his head to one side and shut one eye as if he were taking aim at something Traveler couldn't see. Then he started to laugh, keeping it up until coughing got the better of him.

After a while he said, "Joe Smith was a handsome man, but those Children are a scruffy-looking lot, especially the elders. I can't see their appeal, that's for sure, but every time you see them, women are hanging all over them. Some of those women are young and good-looking, too, for Christ's sake. Go take a look for yourselves, if you don't believe me.''

He grinned. "My Erma would have cut off my balls if I'd tried taking another wife.''

Laughter started him coughing again.

"Is there anything I can get you?'' Martin asked.

Moffit waved Martin back into his chair. When the spasms subsided, he popped a pill in his mouth, chewed and swallowed, then leaned back in his chair and closed his eyes.

"If we wanted to talk to those elders, who would we ask for?'' Martin said.

"If I gave you a couple of names, I wouldn't want you to use mine.'' His voice rasped. "What the hell am I thinking about. Use my name all you want. They'd be doing me a favor if they hurried me along to my Emma. Horace Snelgrove and Orrin Porter, they're the big shots. Earl Hillman sort of hangs on in third place.''

Traveler and Martin exchanged glances. Vonda Hillman was the woman jailed in the county seat, charged with attempting to kill Jason Thurgood.

"Tell us about Hillman's wife,'' Martin said.

Moffit slapped his knee. "I love it. I can see you two are going to be a pain in the ass around here. And yes, she's the one who shot Thurgood. I wasn't there myself, you understand, but those who were, friends I've known most of my life, say it was one of God's miracles. They say His hand reached out and caught that bullet in midair.''

"Vonda Hillman,'' Traveler prompted.

"I thought she was a good, God-fearing Mormon until she took that shot. Earl was too, until he took up with Moroni's Children.''

"What do you hear about a woman named Liz Smoot?''

Moffit slapped his knee again. "Come to think, I'm not going to die just yet. I'm going to stick around for a while and watch the fun. But take my advice. I don't care who you are, watch out for the one calling himself Orrin Porter. Don't be fooled by the looks of him either. He's sneaky and mean, and he's a bully."

He grinned at Traveler. "Just let me live long enough to see you beat the shit out of him. That's all I ask. Then God can call me home."

He shooed them out of the lean-to. "Ruth will be waiting dinner for you by now."

FOURTEEN

Ruth Holcomb's house was two stories of bleak red brick, pure Utah Gothic as Martin called it, though technically it was a pioneer variant of Victorian Eclectic. Houses like it had sprung up throughout Utah during the 1890s, tall narrow structures, with arched churchlike windows and steeply pitched roofs. They had no front porch to speak of, only a concrete stoop. This one differed from its neighbors only because of the small patch of carefully tended grass in the front yard.

The smell of freshly baked bread overwhelmed Traveler the moment Ruth opened her door. Martin, who was ahead of him on the stoop, went up on tiptoe to say, "I think I'm in love."

Shaking her head at him, she stepped back to let them inside. "You men didn't have to knock. I don't lock the doors until the sun goes down. Before the Children moved in, I never locked them at all. Now I might as well live in Provo or some other big city."

Traveler, who was carrying the cat's paraphernalia, had to duck to get through the pioneer-size doorway.

"Dinner's just about to go on the table," she told them. "I'll show you to your rooms so you can wash up before we eat. Your cat's on the service porch and needs that litter box you're carrying."

"His name is Brigham," Traveler said.

She raised an eyebrow but said nothing as she led them through a small cramped living room filled with well-worn, comfortable furniture and into a steamy aroma-filled kitchen. On the service porch, reached through a connecting door, Brigham lay curled on top of the washing machine. Newspapers, soggy in spots, covered the linoleum floor around the machine.

"I put down some of my newspaper articles for him," she said. "It's about all they're good for. In case you didn't know, I'm a stringer for the Salt Lake paper. These days, all they want are features, nothing about what's killing everybody here in Downwind."

"We saw the town's name change at city hall," Traveler said.

She looked pleased. "If the council won't vote for an official alteration, I say spray paint is the next best thing."

As soon as Brigham's litter box was in place, she showed Traveler and Martin to the stairway at the back of the kitchen. At the top of the stairs, two side-by-side bedrooms, large enough only for a double bed and a three-drawer pine bureau, were tucked under the eaves. The only place Traveler could stand without slouching was the center of the room, directly beneath the ceiling's peak. The rooms shared what had been a single closet now remodeled into a compact bathroom.

Rising heat mixing with the smell of bread and roast beef made the attic like an oven. Underlying the aroma of food was the furniture's beeswax polish.

"Don't worry about the heat," Ruth said as if reading Traveler's mind. "We get a breeze as soon as the sun goes down." She opened the window in one room and then the other.

"We can bunk together," Martin said when she'd finished.

"We wouldn't want to take your bedroom."

"I've got a sofa bed downstairs. That's where I usually sleep anyway in summertime."

As soon as she'd left them alone, Traveler tested the bed, which squeaked under his weight but felt firm enough. At bed level he could feel cooler air coming from the open window, though sunset was still a good hour away. Nightstands flanked the bed, a gooseneck reading lamp on one, an extension phone on the other.

"Tomorrow we go looking for the Smoot woman," Martin said.

"If we do that, they'll know we've been hired by her father. Better we stick to Thurgood as ordered."

"Ellsworth may have told you one thing but meant another."

"What do you think he meant?" Traveler said.

"Even church apostles know better than to concern themselves with messiahs, especially when they have something more important to worry about, like a daughter and grandson hanging out with polygamists."

"I think it's time we called Willis Tanner for a little clarification."

"Talk to him about that damned clinic while you're at it."

After asking for permission to use the phone, Traveler called Willis Tanner at home, collect.

"No church business," Tanner said immediately. "Not on the phone unless it's a secure line at my office."

Martin, who had his head next to Traveler's so he could listen in, grabbed the receiver. "Everybody in town already seems to know our business, so talking about it won't hurt."

"Do they know who you're working for?"

"Use your head," Martin said. "Damn near everybody in this state knows who Liz Smoot's father is."

"I'm hanging up," Tanner said.

Traveler took back the phone. "Not before you get us some information."

87

"I told you before—"

"The Echo Canyon Clinic, Willis. I want everything you can get."

"That's the federal government. I don't have access."

"Sure, Willis. And church security and the Danites are a myth."

Tanner sighed. "How soon do you need it?"

"Tomorrow will be fine." Traveler recited Ruth Holcomb's telephone number. "You can leave a message with our landlady if we're not here."

"Why anybody named you after an angel, I'll never know," Tanner said and hung up.

When Traveler and Martin went downstairs ten minutes later, a platter of roast beef stood at the head of the kitchen table waiting to be carved. Next to it bowls of mashed potatoes, parsnips, a lime Jell-O molded salad, and a loaf of unsliced bread had been set out on a white tablecloth, along with Sunday best china, gleaming silverware, and large wineglasses filled with lemonade.

A breeze, accentuated by cross ventilation between the kitchen windows and a back screen door, made the atmosphere bearable. An apple pie was cooling on one of the windowsills.

"Parsnips were a tradition with my wife's family," Martin said. "Kary's people kept them in the root cellar so they could eat them year round."

"I recognize that look on your face," Ruth said, smiling. "As a child, I wore it every Sunday when I sat down to dinner. But this isn't a pioneer recipe, I promise you." She placed a knife and a sharpener next to the platter.

She'd exchanged the man's shirt she'd been wearing earlier for a light blue sleeveless blouse with ruffles down the front that both camouflaged her breasts and emphasized them at the same time. "Now who's going to do the carving?"

Martin said, "It's a father's duty to pass traditions on to his son. So go ahead, Mo. We'll see how much you've learned. Besides, his mother used to say he was a natural-born doctor with a surgeon's touch."

Grimacing, Traveler stropped the knife, then sliced through the meat easily.

"I'm impressed," Ruth told him.

"You have me to thank," Martin said. "I've taught him everything he knows."

Traveler served meat onto the waiting plates and then passed them around. When everyone had added their own vegetables, Ruth lowered her head. "For this food, Lord, and for this company, we thank you. Amen."

Gingerly, Traveler tasted the parsnips. Kary's recipe had called for frying in Crisco until blackened. Ruth's hinted at brown sugar and reminded him of Thanksgiving yams, though more subtle in flavor. He looked up from his plate to find her watching him.

"Well?" she asked.

"My mother would have been jealous."

Ruth sampled the parsnips for herself.

"We talked to Hanna Eccles and Ben Moffit this afternoon," Martin said matter-of-factly.

"I know. The word's around town. I heard it from Norm Shipler, who runs the general store. I hope you don't mind, but he said he wanted to drop by here later tonight and see you two. 'After dark,' he said, so it must be important. Norm gets up with the chickens and goes to bed with them too."

"Did he say why?" Traveler asked.

"I don't think it's dry goods he has on his mind."

Traveler finished his parsnips before returning to the subject that Martin had begun. "Hanna and Ben don't seem taken with your new arrivals here in town."

"Are you talking about the Children or Jason Thurgood?"

"Both, I guess."

Abruptly she tilted her head to one side and eyed Traveler through half-closed eyes. "What is it you really want to know, Mr. Traveler?"

"What do you know about Jason Thurgood?"

Ruth busied herself ladling out second helpings of parsnips. That done, she fetched a pitcher of lemonade from the kitchen counter and refilled their glasses. Her flushed face glistened with sweat.

"To answer your question, I've written an article about him for the paper. I could ask you to wait for publication and read it for yourself, but I don't think you're here to steal my story. There's not much to it, really. I don't know if he works miracles or not. But I think we're lucky to have a real doctor here in town finally, not that he can do anything for us downwinders."

At that moment Traveler felt the draft intensify from the open window behind him. He turned in time to see the Furnace Mountains catch fire in the setting sun.

"That's the evening breeze I told you about," Ruth said.

She left the table and went outside. Traveler and Martin followed her through the screen door and out onto the newly mown grass.

Only the mountain's highest peaks burned now, fired by a last sliver of sun. When that sank beneath the horizon, all color faded. The wind turned cold immediately.

Ruth, standing in a patch of light spilling from the kitchen window, shivered. "My husband didn't like sunsets. He said it was like watching death. Sunrises were birth, he said."

A voice spoke from the darkness. "Ruth, it's me, Norm Shipler. Would you turn out the light so I can come in."

"No one's watching," she said.

"Please."

Out of the corner of his eye, Traveler caught Martin's movement. Though his father was well out of the light, the practiced gesture was recognizable enough, his .45 automatic being returned to its hiding place beneath a loose fitting shirt.

"Stay out here until I cut the pie," Ruth told Shipler, "then I'll pull the shades and you can come in and have a piece with us."

"I'd like to speak to the men alone, if you don't mind."

She sighed but didn't object.

Five minutes later, with only the glow of the propane burner under the coffee pot to light the kitchen, Shipler slipped into the chair Ruth had been using. He was a spindly man, nearly emaciated, whose bones showed, particularly in his face.

"Do you know who I am?" Shipler said.

"You own the general store," Martin answered.

"It's not mine, not anymore. At least, not so you'd know it. Horace Snelgrove and Orrin Porter run it and everything in this town. But they're afraid of you. I could see it in their faces today."

"We haven't met them," Martin said.

"They saw you, I guess, because I heard them talking about you. They said you looked like trouble and that probably the church sent you to spy on them. Is that true?"

"We're not here to investigate Moroni's Children," Martin said.

Shipler sucked a quick breath. "Then I'll hire you to do it. I want them out of here and out of my life. I have two daughters, Eula and Vyrle. They've taken up with Porter and I want them back."

"How old are they?" Traveler said.

"Old enough so I can't have him arrested, if that's what you mean. Even if they were underage, Marshal Peake wouldn't go up against the likes of Porter. That's why I came to you. I've got ten thousand dollars squirreled away in a Salt Lake bank. It's yours if you get rid of the Children. I don't care how you do it. Bury them in the desert as far as I'm concerned. No questions asked."

"I'm sorry," Traveler said. "We have another job to do. Even if we didn't, I don't see what we could do for you legally."

91

"God help me, then." Shipler knocked his chair over as he stood up. "God help you, too."

At the sound of the screen door slamming behind him, Ruth returned to the kitchen, switched on the light, and returned the chair to an upright position.

"It's always the same, isn't it?" she said as she sat down. "Men sending women out of the room. 'For your own good,' they tell us. 'Or we can't speak freely in front of you, we can't swear.' What do they think we are, breakable like china?"

"Women never left the room when I asked them to," Martin said.

"My husband sent me out of the room just before he died. It was for my own good, the nurse told me later. He didn't want me to see him suffering." She shook her head. "It was a betrayal."

FIFTEEN

That's some woman downstairs," Martin said, slipping into bed beside Traveler.

Traveler moved over in the cramped bed until he was against the wall. "In case you've forgotten, we're paying for both rooms."

"There's no use dirtying the sheets and making extra work for her."

"Let's hope we're not making trouble for her by just being in her house."

"I have a feeling she can take care of herself."

Traveler rose up on one elbow and stared at his father. "You always did like widows."

"It's not me she has her eyes on."

"You're imagining things."

Martin shook his head. "Our luck with women had to change someday. Your luck this time."

"Turn off the light."

"Two wise men like us in search of a messiah need all the light they can get."

"Kill the light."

The moment it was dark the phone rang downstairs.

"This time of night it has to be for us," Martin said.

A moment later Traveler heard Ruth Holcomb on the stairs. Halfway up, she called, "Mr. Traveler, a phone call for you."

"Which one?" Martin asked.

"He says his name is Barney Chester. He's calling from Salt Lake and asked for Moroni Traveler."

"I'll be right there." Traveler climbed over the end of the bed and turned on the light. Since he hadn't brought either pajamas or a robe, he slipped on yesterday's jeans and shirt and went downstairs barefooted.

Ruth, wearing a fuzzy bathrobe and a freshly scrubbed look, showed him to the phone on the kitchen wall next to the sink before returning to her sofa bed. She caught him admiring her bare calves before he picked up the receiver and said, "Is something wrong, Barney?"

"You're damn right. Bill and Charlie are driving me crazy."

"I'm three hundred miles away," Traveler reminded him.

"They said you gave them the money, Mo. They bought one of those backyard wading pools, brought it into my lobby and inflated the damned thing."

"That was eating money I gave them."

"The next thing I knew, they filled it with water and started dunking themselves. One baptism for each of their dead relatives, or so they said. I think they'd been smoking some of Charlie's medicine, because they'd stripped naked and the water was ice cold."

Traveler sighed. "How did you know where to find me, Barney?"

"I got the marshal's office from information. He gave me this number."

"This is a private residence," Traveler said, glancing at Ruth apologetically. He was sorry to see that those firm legs of hers were now covered by a comforter.

Chester said, "They slopped so much water around that I slipped on the floor and damn near killed myself when I tried to throw them out. Nephi Bates called the cops, figuring I was dead, then tried to get Bill and Charlie arrested for sacrilege."

"You must have hit your head, Barney, because there's nothing I can do from here."

"I have few enough tenants in my building as it is. If I lose any more, I won't be able to pay the taxes."

"All right. Put them on the phone and I'll talk to them."

"You're right, Mo. That's what I should have done. But I was in pain. I wasn't thinking straight when I let them go. My head's still throbbing."

Traveler stretched the phone cord to its limit to sit at the kitchen table. There, he was out of Ruth's line of sight, though he could still see her reflection in the glass panel of a pioneer breakfront. She was sitting up against the back of the sofa, arms folded across her breasts, the picture of impatience. "Barney, I can hear it coming like a freight train. What did you do?"

"It's their own fault, Moroni. They ran out of relatives to baptize, and that's when Charlie said they ought to go on a mission to Indian reservations. There, he said, they'd find plenty of souls in need of raising. So I gave them the money to make the trip."

"Where, Barney?"

"That's why I'm calling you this time of night. I couldn't send them to the middle of nowhere, could I?"

Traveler groaned.

"You've got to understand, Mo. I had to get them out of here. Even then, it took me and Nephi an hour to mop the floor after we got that damned pool drained and deflated."

"Answer the question, Barney."

"You're in Fire Creek, right? Southern Utah. A prime area for Indian sites, Charlie says."

"Charlie's a Navajo in case you haven't noticed. The nearest reservation here is Shivwits."

"He says there are souls all over that area in need of raising and that you and Martin are destined to help them."

"We're working, Barney."

"They're on the bus right now. It arrives in St. George at midnight."

"For Christ's sake." Traveler covered the receiver with his hand. "Mrs. Holcomb, how long will it take me to drive to St. George at this time of night?"

"Four or five hours, at least, maybe six. Myself, I wouldn't try it in the dark."

Traveler relayed the information to Chester.

"Sorry, Moroni. I didn't know you were with a woman."

"Do they have enough money for a hotel?"

"The pool took everything they had, Bill told me. I bought them a couple of sandwiches for the trip and gave them ten bucks spending money, but that's all I could manage other than the bus tickets."

Traveler checked the kitchen clock. It was closer to eleven than ten. "I can't be in St. George before dawn."

"They'll wait in the depot until you get there."

"Can you imagine Bill and Charlie in small-town Utah?" Traveler said. "Chances are they'll get themselves tarred and feathered."

"St. George has grown. California money has come in."

"What were they wearing?"

"The usual. Bill in his robe and Charlie in his disciple outfit."

Which translated as a buckskin shirt, jeans, a cowboy hat and boots, and a medicine bag bulging with Charlie's own spiritual mixture. Martin claimed it was mostly tobacco spiked with marijuana and peyote. Whatever it was, Traveler had hallucinated for hours following an accidental sip of Charlie's so-called mulled wine.

"What about the sandwich boards?" Traveler asked.

"Give me some credit, Mo. I locked them up for safekeeping. I hope you're not mad at me."

"You wouldn't want me to lie, would you?"

"Okay, Mo. I got pissed off and lost my head. But we can't leave Bill and Charlie stranded."

"We?"

"You're closer to St. George than I am."

"That's the first sense you've made," Traveler said and hung up.

Ruth appeared in the kitchen doorway. "If you're going to make that drive, I'd better fix you some strong Postum."

Mormon coffee, Traveler thought, but kept it to himself. The Word of Wisdom: no caffeine, no tobacco, but no mention of wife count.

"That'll be fine," he said and went upstairs to get dressed.

When Martin heard the reason for Chester's call, he offered to make the drive himself. "While I'm gone," he added, "you'd have some time alone with the widow Holcomb."

"Your night vision isn't what it used to be."

"My eyes are good enough to spot a good-looking woman. I hope you've noticed those legs of hers."

Traveler concentrated on his shoelaces.

"Rounded calves," Martin rhapsodized, "heavy but not fat, with trim ankles. Imagine them wrapped around you."

"That's not going to make sleeping any easier. Besides, I thought you liked bony women."

"That's your hang-up, not mine."

"Kary was stick thin."

"And what about your last girlfriend, Claire."

"She wasn't bony when I met her."

"So tell Ruth you need a navigator and take her with you to St. George."

"Some date that would be, taking her to meet Bill and Charlie."

"Take my advice," Martin said. "As soon as you get to St. George, buy them bus tickets and send them back to Barney."

"I think Barney's at the end of his rope."

"You can't bring them here, not while we're working."

"I'll call you from St. George," Traveler said.

"Postum's ready," Ruth called from the bottom of the stairs.

Martin got out of bed, wrapped a blanket around his shoulders, and headed for the stairs, "Not to worry. I'll keep the widow company while you're gone."

SIXTEEN

Brigham Young ordered St. George colonized in 1861 as a southern outpost against invasion from California. Still fresh in his mind was the religious persecution and murder that had driven him and his people out of Nauvoo, Illinois, sending them on a forced march across the continent in 1847. What he hadn't counted on in St. George was the building of the interstate a century later, and with it a flood of cash-rich Californians in search of condominiums and a mild winter climate.

But these days, tourists migrated farther north in August. As for Traveler, he started sweating the moment the sun rose. Too much truck-stop coffee and no sleep made his hand shake as he switched on the Jeep's air conditioner. He cruised the streets looking for the bus terminal. What he found eventually was a drop-off point in front of the Ramada, with only a bus bench to mark the spot. The bench was occupied by a uniformed doorman reading a newspaper. At Traveler's approach, he folded his paper and stood up to open the door.

Traveler waved him back to his seat. "I'm looking for a couple of friends who were dropped off here last night."

"The Salt Lake bus?"

Traveler nodded.

"I wasn't on duty myself, but I heard about it from one of the cops who cruise by here late every night for a look-see."

Traveler swallowed a groan.

"You have to understand. This is a bus stop only, an accommodation. If people don't want to stay at the hotel, we encourage them to move on."

"Where did my friends move to?"

Deliberately, the man raised his wrist to peer at his watch. Traveler recognized the request and handed him a five-dollar bill.

"After they left here, they were picked up in the local cemetery, the cop told me. Skunk drunk, he said."

"Where are they now?"

"Where else, jail."

The duty sergeant at the police building smiled politely. "Bail has been set at twelve hundred and fifty dollars apiece. They didn't look like the kind who'd have friends or it would have been higher."

"What have they been charged with?" Traveler asked.

The policeman's smile broadened. "Bail would have to be in cash, you understand, no checks."

"Is there a bail bondsman in town?"

"Not one who'd touch those two."

"You still haven't told me the charge."

"For twenty-five hundred you can take them away and not come back. It would be better that way, actually. If we have to go to trial, the newspaper will raise hell about desecrating the cemetery. If that happens, who knows what kind of sentence they might get. People get pretty damned upset having their ancestors pissed on.''

"Bill and Charlie aren't that crazy.''

The sergeant shrugged. "That's what the report says. Also they were in possession of an illegal substance.''

"Peyote is legal for Indians.''

"The big guy says he's some kind of prophet. We get too many of them around here as it is.''

Traveler clenched his teeth. The banks didn't open for another two hours. Even when they did, he wasn't certain he had leeway enough on his credit cards to raise twenty-five hundred. If necessary, he'd use the church card that Josiah Ellsworth had provided.

"I'd like to speak with them,'' he said.

"Normally I'd say no at this time of the morning, but I know your name and figure you're good for the money. I don't want you to think we're a bunch of rednecks when you see your friends. They got banged up resisting arrest, pure and simple.''

Viewed through the bars of the cell, Bill had one eye swollen shut and two fingers of his right hand taped together in a makeshift splint. One sleeve of his prophet's robe hung in shreds, the other was missing entirely. Charlie looked untouched except for his missing medicine bag.

"We were baptizing the dead,'' Bill said as soon as the duty sergeant moved out of earshot.

"By pissing on them?''

"It was only beer, Moroni. I swear it.''

Traveler looked to Charlie, who nodded. "Right out of the bottle, no kidneys involved.''

"We didn't have any sacramental wine,'' Bill said. "So I blessed the beer. An impromptu baptism in God's name, what's the harm in that?''

"They want twenty-five hundred for the two of you.''

"Not to worry, Mo," Bill said. "Our religious freedom is at stake. They won't dare bring us to trial."

"You should have waited for me at the bus stop."

"They ran us off."

"All the way to the cemetery?" Traveler said.

"We had money enough for a couple of beers. After that . . ." Bill shrugged.

Charlie said, "We were looking for a place to sleep. How were we to know they patrolled the cemetery."

"As soon as the banks open, I'll get some money," Traveler said. "After that, I'm putting you on the next bus back to Salt Lake."

Bill shook his head. "Charlie and I have been talking. He must visit his ancestors, he says. He must go back to the reservation. He must seek his roots."

"And you, Bill?"

Bill looked at Charlie who folded his arms over his chest and closed his eyes.

"In the end," Bill said, "we must all make such journeys alone. Until he reaches his destination, I will stay with him, making certain that God provides."

"I'm the one doing the providing," Traveler said.

"God is working through you, Moroni."

"Where will you go if I bail you out?"

Charlie opened his eyes. "Eventually the Navajo reservation over in San Juan County."

"That's on the other side of the state."

"For now, we will go with you to the Shivwits reservation near Fire Creek."

Traveler stepped back from the bars. "I'll be back as soon as I can."

"I'm going to need a new robe for the trip," Bill called after him.

Traveler used a pay phone outside the police station to call Ruth Holcomb's number, apologizing immediately for waking her so early.

"We've been up for hours," she said. "Martin and I had breakfast, then went for a walk while it was still cool."

"Could I speak with him, please."

"He's gone off with Jason Thurgood."

"What?"

"Relax, Mr. Traveler. If you're worried about your father running into trouble, don't."

"I should be there backing him up."

"Being with Jason is as good as having an armed escort around here," Ruth said.

"What the hell is going on?"

"Jason heard you were in town asking questions about him, and *no*, I wasn't the one who told him. So he dropped by to supply the answers, as he put it. He and your father got along so well, Martin took him up on the offer to visit a sick shepherd up in the hills."

Traveler didn't like it, but there was nothing he could do except make threats. "If you see Thurgood, tell him I'm holding him personally responsible for my father's safety."

"I'm sure he knows that already," Ruth said, "what with word about you all over town."

"When my father gets back, tell him that I'm going to stop off in Parowan."

"To see Karl Cederlof?"

Traveler sighed. "Yes."

"Moroni's Children ran him out of town when they decided to squat on his land."

"What else should I know?"

"That you'll have to hurry if you want to get back here by dinnertime. I'm making one of your father's favorites, pineapple up-side-down cake. By the way, I took a call for you. Someone named Tanner. He said he was a friend of yours and told me to tell you that he'd call again.''

"I asked him to leave a message.''

"I offered to take one, but he said what he had to say was too complicated and, to use his words, 'strictly confidential.' ''

SEVENTEEN

From St. George, with Bill and Charlie smelling of disinfectant as they slept in the backseat, Traveler headed north on I-15, back-tracking through Cedar City to the old highway, 143. There he turned east to Parowan, seat of Iron County, which was tucked against the base of the Hurricane Cliffs.

Known as the Mother of the South, Parowan stood at the edge of the Dixie National Forest, at an altitude of six thousand feet. It looked too small to be a county seat. The population, according to the city limits sign, was 1,836. Traveler figured 1,500 was more like it.

Karl Cederlof lived behind a chain-link fence topped by rolled razor wire. Traveler parked well back from a gate that was secured with a heavy chain and padlock. Sunk into concrete next to the gate was a six-inch iron post, curved at the top to hold a brass bell.

The house was like everything else in town, built of pink adobe reaped from the red soil. A good-size screened porch had been added, along with iron grilles that covered the two front windows and a sturdy-looking metal storm door. Bill and Charlie woke up the moment Traveler opened the car door.

"Do you want us to come with you?" Bill said.

Traveler shook his head. "There's beer in the cooler, though it may be warm by now."

Charlie automatically reached for his missing medicine bag, which had been confiscated by the St. George police. Both he and Bill claimed that its contents were part of their church ritual, for spiking the sacramental jug Barney kept on hand for them at the Chester Building. Beer was part of their sacrament only when nothing stronger was available.

"When we reach the reservation, my brothers will replenish us," Charlie said.

Wearily, Traveler got out of the car, wedged a business card between one of the chain links and rang the bell. Before the echo faded, the storm door banged open and out rushed two frenzied rottweilers. By the time they'd covered the hundred feet or so from the house to the fence, they'd snarled enough froth to look rabid.

Traveler backed up a step. Behind him, Bill and Charlie rolled up the windows despite the oppressive heat. Traveler stood his ground, keeping his empty hands in plain sight. Sweat began running into his eyes but he made no move to wipe them.

The rottweilers gave up snarling to pace back and forth. A moment later their tails wagged when the storm door opened again and a man came out, a short-barreled shotgun cradled in one arm. He snapped his fingers and the dogs sat.

"I'm looking for Karl Cederlof," Traveler called.

"You've found him." Cederlof came up behind the dogs and stopped. He was a tall man, six-two at least, with stooped shoulders that seemed to apologize for his height. He was wearing a wide-brimmed straw cowboy hat that shaded his eyes from the sun.

"I'm a private investigator," Traveler told him, blinking

against the sweat. "I stuck my card in your fence if you'd care to read it."

Cederlof retrieved it without taking his eyes off Traveler. He didn't look at it until he was behind the dogs again. "Moroni Traveler," he read loudly. "Is this one of Orrin Porter's fucking jokes?" His tone of voice brought the dogs to their feet.

Slowly, Moroni raised his hands. "I have nothing to do with Moroni's Children."

"Easy," Cederlof told the dogs.

"The fact is, I've been hired to look into the situation in Fire Creek and since I'm told you own much of the land around there, I thought it might help if I spoke with you."

"Who hired you?"

"I'm sorry. That's confidential."

"What do you want to talk about?"

"We can start with Moroni's Children."

"They're squatting on my land, did they tell you that? I signed a paper saying those people could live in my houses and on my land rent free. Ever since, I've been waiting for the day that bastard Porter shows up again with another paper in his hand, deeding him everything, including my soul.

"Did you ever look in that man's eyes?" he continued. "He smiles at you. His lips curl, but you can see he wants you dead. When he smiled at me I told him he could have everything, lock, stock, and barrel. 'Where do I sign?' I said. 'I'll deed it over to you right now.' You know what he said to that? 'It won't be necessary. Land only encumbers a man.' He laughed then, looking me up and down. Measuring me for a coffin, I thought."

To keep him talking, Traveler tried a sympathetic smile.

"I thought it was all bullshit before I met him," Cederlof went on, "all that talk about him being the reincarnation of Orrin Porter Rockwell. Another bogeyman to scare kids, I thought, then I saw him for myself. Besides, that land's not worth a damn anymore, what with the radiation and the cancer. Nobody's willing to graze the land or drink milk from Fire Creek cows.''

''Maybe Porter's all bluff,'' Traveler suggested.

''Tell that to Mayor Gibbs, when you find his body.''

''Could we move out of the sun?''

''If you want to keep talking, we stay right here.''

Using one hand, Traveler pulled up his shirt far enough to wipe his eyes. ''Why are you willing to tell me all this?''

''Because when I saw you standing out here, I realized I was a dead man anyway, if that's what Porter wants. The fence can keep the dogs in but it can't keep bullets out.''

Without uncradling his shotgun, Cederlof knelt down to scratch one panting dog and then the other. ''All right,'' he said. ''Home.''

They wagged their tails, then trotted back to the house and disappeared under the porch.

''It's the coolest spot around,'' Cederlof said, ''and there's water for them, too. I rigged up their own faucet under the house. All they have to do is nudge it with their noses.''

''I could use a drink myself.''

Cederlof shook his head, though Traveler had the feeling it had nothing to do with Traveler's comment. ''Mayor Gibbs drove up here to see me a week or so before the election. He said he was thinking of moving out of Fire Creek and wanted to check out Parowan for himself. But that wasn't the real purpose of his visit, no, sir. 'Brother Cederlof,' he says to me, 'since you were the only one in town with brains enough to get out rather than face off with these people, I thought I'd ask your advice.' That wasn't like Jake Gibbs to start doubting himself or asking for advice either. Of course, the cancer had a hold of him by then, that's for sure. Anyway, he says to me, 'Did this guy Porter do everything but make threats?' When I said no, he tells me what's going on. Porter had come to him just like to me, with a smile on his face and a paper in his hand. Only this time he wants Mayor Jake to resign from office and withdraw from the election. For ill health, the paper said.''

Behind the fence, Cederlof paced back and forth, stopping now and then to kick at red rocks. When one of them rolled halfway to the house, a rottweiler's head appeared from beneath the porch, its growl loud enough to carry all the way to Traveler.

Cederlof waved to the dog, who disappeared again. ''Mayor Gibbs laughed in Porter's face. That's what the mayor told me anyway. 'Brother Cederlof,' he said, 'the joke's on him. I would have been out of Fire Creek a long time ago if my health had been good. As it is, there's no way I'm going to resign. If I did that, there wouldn't be anything to do but sit on my front porch and wait for the cancer to eat up what's left of me.' ''

Cederlof sighed deeply. ''All of us are afraid of something, Mr. Traveler. You, me, the dogs. It's just a matter of finding that fear. 'Do you have a secret fear?' Mayor Jake asked me that last time we talked.''

He paused to glance over his shoulder. '' 'With me,' I told him, 'it's dentists. I'd do anything to stop them drilling my teeth.' When I asked Jake what frightened him most he said, 'When I wouldn't sign the paper, Orrin Porter told me he knew my worst nightmare. How he knew I don't know. But he did.' ''

Cederlof shuddered. '' 'Worse than a dentist's drill?' I asked him. He never answered, but he didn't have to. I saw the fear in his face. 'Don't be a fool,' I told him. 'Resign.' I would have. I'll tell you one thing. If Porter shows up here, I'll sign anything. You can be sure of that.''

''Then why bother with the fence and the dogs?''

''How do I know he'll come with a paper in his hand? If he's coming with a dentist's drill, I want enough warning to put a bullet in my head.''

EIGHTEEN

By the time Traveler got back on the interstate heading south toward St. George, Bill and Charlie had finished the beer and were singing in the back seat.

"I'm out in Utah in the Mormon land,
I'm not coming home, 'cause I'm a-living grand.
I used to rave about a single life,
Now every day I get a brand-new wife."

When the verse ended, Charlie said, "I am going home. The nearest reservation will do."

"It's not on the way," Traveler told him. "And I told you before, it's not Navajo."

"We can pick up the old Highway 8 out of St. George."

In the rearview mirror, Traveler saw Charlie put an arm around Bill.

"From the Shivwits reservation," Charlie said, "I can show

you where to pick up a back way into Fire Creek.''

Bill nodded. ''It sounds good to me, Mo. You can drop us off while you and Martin do your work and then pick us up on your way home. That way we'd be out of your hair.''

An hour ago Traveler would have jumped at the suggestion, but that was before he'd spoken with Karl Cederlof.

''I don't have time for detours. Martin doesn't have anyone covering his back.''

''What did that guy back there say to get you so worked up?''

Instead of answering, Traveler only shook his head. For all he knew Cederlof was crazy, the victim of nothing more than nasty smiles and veiled threats. Even so, Traveler hadn't doubted him for a moment when he said he'd put a bullet in his own head rather than fall into the hands of a man claiming to be the reincarnation of Orrin Porter Rockwell.

Bill said, ''Martin always says he covers your back.''

Traveler clenched his teeth, checked the mirror for signs of the Highway Patrol, then gradually increased his speed. Fifteen minutes later, he exited I-15 at St. George and stopped at the first public phone he could find. It was late afternoon, time for Sunday dinner.

Ruth Holcomb answered after one ring.

''It's Moroni Traveler. Let me speak to my father.''

''He's come and gone. He's spending the night with Jason Thurgood, 'under the stars,' they said, 'sitting around a bonfire.' ''

Traveler took a deep breath to keep from banging the receiver against the wall. Keeping your back covered was one of Martin's rules of survival, right up there with the avoidance of church entanglements.

''My father wouldn't take off like that,'' Traveler said.

''He told me you'd say that. But you haven't met Jason Thurgood. When you do, you'll understand why he and your father hit it off so well.''

"Where's Orrin Porter?"

"I don't know. I expected to see him, what with people saying that he likes to keep an eye on Thurgood, especially when Jason spends the night in the desert."

Traveler pounded the side of his hand against the wall of the booth hard enough to dent the metal. "Who else is on this so-called pilgrimage?"

"I don't know. I didn't ask. Your father seemed perfectly happy with the arrangements."

"I'll be there in two hours."

"It won't do your father any good if you run off the road somewhere."

Traveler took another deep breath. His lungs had that burning sensation that came after a long run.

Behind him a car door slammed. He glanced back to see Bill and Charlie out of the car and standing in the shade of a spindly piñon pine. If he took them with him that would be two more backs to cover, but if he detoured to the reservation, God knew how long it would take him to reach Fire Creek.

He checked the sun. "I should be there before dark," he told Ruth.

"I'll keep dinner warm," she said and hung up.

Traveler rounded up Bill and Charlie and headed west on St. George Boulevard toward the center of town. He bypassed the Four Seasons Inn, whose tennis courts and lavish swimming pool looked too grand for the likes of Bill and Charlie, and settled on the Zion Rest Motel. To forestall any check-in problems, Traveler used his church credit card to get them a room. The clerk didn't look happy at the sight of Bill and Charlie, but he didn't argue either, especially when Traveler signed an open-ended receipt in advance.

Traveler made one more stop, a downtown bank where the automated teller accepted the church card and promptly paid out three hundred dollars in crisp twenties. When he divided the cash between Bill and Charlie, they looked worried.

"We already owe you twenty-five hundred," Bill said.

"This is church money."

"Who has to repay it?"

Traveler shrugged.

"We'll accept it as a donation," Bill said.

"We'll use it where it will do the most good, on the reservation," Charlie added.

"You two stay here at the motel," Traveler said. "I'll be back for you as soon as I can."

"There's no need to give us a second thought, Mo. We're right where we want to be, near the souls of Charlie's ancestors."

NINETEEN

Traveler stoked himself with anger and caffeine, drinking one Coke after another on the drive back to Fire Creek. By the time he parked in front of Ruth Holcomb's he had the shakes. So did the Jeep, which had picked up shimmies and a rattle when he hit fifty miles an hour on the last stretch of corrugated dirt road. The inside of the vehicle, like Traveler, was coated with red grit.

Stopping short of the front steps, he raised a dust cloud trying to brush himself off. He was wiping his hands on the grass when the screen door banged open and Ruth Holcomb came out to greet him.

"I ought to turn the hose on you," Ruth said, looking cool in her red shorts and baggy T-shirt. She smiled, trying to make a joke out of her comment, but her eyes betrayed her. Something was wrong.

Traveler clenched his fists. "Is Martin all right?"

She laid a restraining hand on his arm, confirming his instincts. "I could tell you were upset on the phone, so I did some asking around in town. It comes to this. Many of the Children fear for Jason's safety. I do too sometimes, because of all the rival cults in this part of the state. They'd like nothing better than to bring down Moroni's Children. Which is why the Children look after Jason so carefully, especially when he goes into the desert. 'Like a prophet from the Bible,' Orrin Porter told me when I found him down at Shipler's. 'But these days a prophet needs a bodyguard. So we watch over Jason from a distance, taking turns.' "

"You said *we*," Traveler pointed out.

"I'm not a member of the Children, but I'm one of Jason's fans."

"You're trying to tell me that Orrin Porter is out there watching him, aren't you?"

She shook her head. "It was his turn, but he declined. He said he didn't think a man like you would understand his intentions."

"He's right."

"Orrin sent both his wives in his place, though if you ask me, he probably wanted them out of the way while he tends to Norm Shipler's daughters, Eula and Vyrle. Porter crooks his finger at them and they roll over, and not just figuratively either." Ruth sighed. "Maybe they're right. Maybe it's best to take your happiness before it's too late. Maybe—"

"Am I missing something?" Traveler interrupted. "If Porter's wives are watching over Jason, I don't see any problem for my father."

"Porter has some kind of hold over those women. I don't trust them. The way they fawn on Orrin makes me blush sometimes. I sure as hell wouldn't turn my back on them."

"If we left now, could we find Thurgood and my father?"

Shading her eyes, Ruth looked west. "Maybe in daylight, but the sun will be down in half an hour. Only a lunatic would wander around in that desert in the dark."

"Where can I find Orrin Porter, then?"

"Your friend Mr. Tanner called again and still wouldn't leave a

115

message. He left two numbers you can call.''

"He can wait. Now tell me where Porter is.''

"Like always, down at Shipler's. Shipler's Video by now, which is what Orrin calls the general store after the regular closing time.''

By the time Traveler walked the block and a half to Shipler's, Marshal Peake was waiting out front, trying to look casual, without succeeding. The two women sitting on the curb in front of Cavin's Feed and Seed across the street weren't having any better luck.

In answer to Traveler's questioning look, Peake raised his hands to waist level, then turned them over palms up like a supplicant. "Ruth Holcomb called me and told me to keep an eye on you."

"And the ladies across the street?"

"Maybe they're keeping an eye on me, though I haven't asked."

Before Traveler could respond, Norm Shipler appeared in the open doorway, leaning heavily on crutches. A cast covered his left leg from hip to toe. He glared at Traveler, shook off an offer of help, and then edged sideways across the threshold and onto the sidewalk, where he rocked momentarily before catching his balance. His face glistened with sweat.

"What happened to you?" Traveler asked him.

Shipler raised one crutch far enough to point it at Traveler. "You did."

"What does that mean?"

"I asked you for help and you turned me down." Shipler readjusted his crutches until his back was to the women across the street. "They've been watching me ever since. The word is I was restocking shelves inside the store when I fell off the ladder. It hurt like a bitch bastard when Jason Thurgood set the break, let me tell you."

"Tell us what really happened," Peake said.

"I don't ask anyone for help, not anymore."

When the marshal reached out to him, Shipler backed up, losing his balance. Traveler caught him under the arms and whispered, "Give me a name."

As Shipler squirmed to break free, all color drained from his face. His chest heaved. "Take my advice, Traveler, and leave town before you get the same treatment I did. 'Doing God's work,' they call it."

"Who?" Traveler asked.

Shipler pushed away from him and lurched down the street. The women opposite made no move to follow.

Traveler stared at the marshal. "What are you going to do?"

"No one ever testifies against the Children."

"Does it work the other way around?"

Peake pulled at his lower lip. "The way I see it, if *you* break someone's leg without a lot of witnesses around, no one's going to say a damned thing, me included."

"Maybe I can get more out of Shipler if I talk to him alone."

"And his fan club across the street?"

By now, Shipler had crossed Fillmore Avenue and was continuing down Main, half a block away. Traveler turned and went after him. At the corner, Traveler stopped abruptly and looked back at the women, who were now on their feet and following on the opposite side of the street. Smiling, he crossed the asphalt toward them. They immediately stopped and pretended to be window shopping, though all the stores along that stretch were boarded up.

"Excuse me," he said to catch their attention. When he had it, he pointed a finger at them and then shook it until they fled back toward the dry goods store.

Traveler caught up with Shipler at the corner of Main and Parowan.

"Are you trying to get me killed?" Shipler asked.

"Hiring me wouldn't have done any good," Traveler said. "I couldn't protect you forever."

"Then why are you here talking to me?"

"I need to know what I'm up against." What Martin was up against, Traveler thought, but didn't say so. "Did Orrin Porter break your leg?"

"I'm not saying yes, I'm not saying no." Hobbling on his crutches, Shipler moved east on Parowan just far enough to be out of sight of Main Street. "Help me sit down, for Christ's sake, before my arms fall off."

Traveler eased him onto the curb and then sat beside him.

"I used to be like Porter, full of juice, wanting damn near every woman I laid eyes on. But I had a conscience. I knew what was right. But Porter . . ." Shipler lowered his head until his chin rested against his breastbone. "I saw them doing it, you know, my own daughters, things I would never have asked my wife to do."

He swallowed so hard Traveler could hear his Adam's apple bob. "If you ask me, Porter set it up so I couldn't help getting an eyeful. A man can't let that pass, you know, not when it's his own daughters. I spent all day working up my courage to confront him. Do you know what he said to me? 'You'd be an unmarked grave out in the desert, old man, if they weren't spreading their legs for me.' His words, to me, their father. Thank God their mother didn't live to hear such things."

"Have you talked to your daughters?" Traveler asked.

Shipler's eyes closed hard enough to squeeze out tears. "The devil has come among us to steal away my baby girls."

" 'For I say unto you that whatever is good cometh from God,' " Traveler said, remembering one of his mother's favorites, " 'and whatsoever is evil cometh from the devil.' "

Shipler raised his head. "You're as green as the rest of them.

'And it came to pass that I beheld this great and abominable church; and I saw the devil that he was the founder of it.' It's clear to me, Mr. Traveler. The Children are the devil's pawns. They follow Jason Thurgood, the devil himself.''

''I'm told he's not a member of Moroni's Children.''

''The Children stayed to themselves until he came. Before Thurgood, they claimed only the desert, not my store. Take it from me. Men like Orrin Porter draw their strength from the devil.''

''I'll keep that in mind.''

Shipler held out his hand until Traveler shook it.

''I took Thurgood by the hand too,'' Shipler said, ''but he wasn't there.''

Kary had been a great one for handshaking, too, a test laid down by Joseph Smith himself. ''If it be the devil,'' Smith decreed, ''when you ask him to shake hands you will feel nothing.''

''Help me up,'' Shipler said. ''I want to be home before dark.''

As soon as Traveler obliged, Shipler hobbled away on his crutches. Watching him, Traveler kept telling himself that the man was crazy. To think otherwise would be to believe that Martin was spending the night with the devil.

TWENTY

The sun had set by the time Traveler retraced his steps to Shipler's General Store. The building reminded him of Depression photographs he'd seen in history books. Its uneven pine plank facade gave the impression that it had been meant as a temporary measure only, something thrown up by pioneers to last through the winter until more permanent materials became available.

Fluorescent light spilled from the open doorway, illuminating Marshal Peake's face as he sat on the hood of a dusty pickup out front. His straw cowboy hat hung on the truck's antenna.

"Well," Peake demanded, "did you get a name?"

"The wrong one, I think."

"Anybody I ought to know about?"

"I'd keep an eye on Shipler, if I were you," Traveler said. "He claims to have seen the devil, or laid a hand on him at least."

"That's just Norm. He's been saying things like that for years. Anybody who crosses him gets the honorary title of Satan." Peake slid off the hood and rocked on the heels of his cowboy boots. "For all we know, maybe he's right. Maybe the devil has moved here to Fire Creek."

"You don't believe that."

"The Children claim to speak for God. God and the devil go together, since you can't have one without the other."

An evening breeze caught the brim of Peake's hat, causing it and the car's antenna to sway back and forth. The marshal's eyes tracked the movement as he spoke. "You know what they're saying around town, don't you? That Orrin Porter ordered Norm Shipler's punishment."

"For what?"

"For talking to you."

"You're talking to me."

"If they come at me, I'll take some of them with me. That's a promise. But there's nothing much the Children can take from me unless they want to go into the gas station business, which doesn't pay spit."

"You're all the law there is," Traveler reminded him.

"Mostly my job is to handle the drunks, and since the Children don't drink, I have very little to do with them, officially."

"And if they break the law right in front of you?"

"There's more than one way to see justice done, Mr. Traveler."

"I have something to say to Mr. Porter inside. If you come in with me, I'll have a witness to whatever happens."

"He's in there all right, behind the counter, along with Horace Snelgrove, who presides over the Children. You can't miss Snelgrove. He dresses in black like Brigham Young."

With a smile, Peake retrieved his hat, tipped it in Traveler's direction, and then ambled up the street, checking doors as he went.

Inside Shipler's, canned laughter boomed from a television set. The laughter turned real the moment Traveler crossed the threshold and banged his knee against the barrel that was propping open the door. Inside the barrel, ax handles rattled.

Refusing to limp, Traveler crossed the threshold. The store looked to be thirty feet deep and maybe half that wide. Floor-to-ceiling shelves, filled with everything from canned goods to work boots, lined the side walls. A waist-high counter ran along the back wall.

The man behind the counter—bone thin, no more than thirty, wearing a white T-shirt with sleeves rolled to the armpits exposing stringy biceps—beckoned Traveler forward. To reach him, Traveler had to thread his way through a crowd of women sitting on the floor facing a large-screen television set that sat on a shelf behind the counter. The women had positioned themselves in a circle around a high, cane-back chair in which Horace Snelgrove sat imperially, dressed in a black broadcloth suit, just as the marshal had said. He'd failed to mention Snelgrove's resemblance to the romantic portraits of Joseph Smith, movie-star handsome, with dark hair and magnetic eyes.

Smiling, Snelgrove turned his head to watch Traveler's approach, while the women continued to stare straight ahead at the screen.

When Traveler reached the counter, Porter raised a welcoming hand in which he held a videocassette. "We were expecting you, Brother Traveler."

"Indeed," Snelgrove added. "We were about to watch a miracle, Brother Traveler. Come, view it with us. Seeing it may change your life."

At Snelgrove's signal, Porter fed the cassette into a VCR and punched the Play button. Traveler saw Jason Thurgood again, the same videotape that the apostle, Josiah Ellsworth, had played for him. Only this time it was in slow motion. The same strange halo-like light surrounded Thurgood as he stood on the crude wooden platform, his shirttails flapping in the wind. This time, in slow-mo, the sound was gone. The women sitting on the floor supplied it, parroting the words exactly as Traveler remembered them.

They all screamed when Vonda Hillman, disheveled and wild-eyed, leapt onto the platform, thrust the revolver against Thurgood's chest, and fired. When Thurgood stumbled backward, the women wailed in unison. When he caught his balance, they sighed with relief. When he touched what should have been a wound and smiled, they murmured, "God's miracle has been shown to us."

Porter stopped the tape. "Have you seen the light, Brother Traveler?"

Traveler glanced back at Snelgrove. The women seemed to have moved more tightly around him. By doing so, they'd cut off Traveler's avenues of escape.

"I have a message," he said.

"From old Norm Shipler, no doubt," Porter mocked.

"From me. I'm holding you personally responsible for my father's safety."

Behind him, Traveler sensed Snelgrove rising to his feet. Shifting his weight, Traveler brought both men into his field of vision.

"Is that a threat, Brother Traveler?" Porter asked.

Traveler nodded. "If something happens to him, it happens to you too."

Snelgrove chuckled. "He's perfectly safe from us."

"Is he safe from Jason Thurgood?"

Snelgrove pointed a finger at Traveler. "If I were you, it wouldn't be my father I was worried about. Jason Thurgood is a man chosen by God. We've shown you proof of that, there on the screen. You have been given a chance, Brother Traveler. You have been shown the path to salvation. If you turn away from it, God will not forgive you."

Porter said, " 'They that fight against Zion and the covenant people of the Lord shall lick up the dust of their feet. For all the people of the Lord are they who wait for the coming of the messiah.' "

"Jason Thurgood," Snelgrove said, "is a man dedicated to helping others, just as we are. He heals their bodies, we tend to their souls. That why we've joined forces. 'We are your army,' we told him. And he welcomed us, as he did your father. A chosen man, your father, because Jason has befriended him. But you?''

Two teenage girls rose from the circle of women and approached Traveler, both smiling at him suggestively.

"Did you come here seeking our women?" Snelgrove asked.

"Like Vyrle here?" Porter added, pointing to one of them. "Or Eula?"

Eula hung on one of Traveler's arms, Vyrle the other.

"We came into this desert," Snelgrove went on, "a place that nonbelievers like yourself might see as a barren wasteland, because God directed us here. We await His pleasure and His messiah.''

"Jason Thurgood?" Traveler asked trying to disengage from the women, but they clung to him tenaciously.

"Brother Thurgood follows God in his own way. We don't intervene. He will come to us, even lead us, if that is God's will.''

"There are some who say he's the messiah," Traveler prompted.

"We listen to God, not gossip. We prayed to God for help and He sent Brother Thurgood into the wilderness to find himself. But he found us also.''

Two more women rose from the ranks around Snelgrove and came toward Traveler.

"Lay hands upon him," Snelgrove told them.

Shyly, the women touched Traveler's hands.

"Do you feel the devil?" Snelgrove asked the women.

They nodded.

Snelgrove shook his head. "You see, Brother Traveler, what we are up against. The power of disbelief. It fills your soul. You are the devil's pawn without even knowing it.''

Despite being surrounded, Traveler felt he could still escape if need be, though he'd have to trample half a dozen women to do it. He said, "What does Thurgood say to all this?"

"Some things don't have to be asked." Snelgrove tapped his chest. "You feel it in here, the path to salvation."

"If you don't mind, I'd like to see Thurgood for myself," Traveler said. "And my father, tonight if possible."

Porter rapped the counter for attention. " 'And it came to pass that there arose a mist of darkness and they that wandered from the path were lost.' "

"You're paraphrasing," Traveler said. " 'Behold, the sword of vengeance hangeth over you, and the time soon cometh that he avengeth the blood of the saints upon you.' "

Snelgrove chuckled. "You know your *Book of Mormon,* Brother Traveler. But the sword is in God's hand, not yours." He extended a palm. "Not even mine, yet."

Orrin Porter came around the counter to lay a small two-way radio in Snelgrove's waiting palm.

"Two of Brother Porter's wives are watching over your father and Jason Thurgood even as we speak. They're devoted women, like my own dear ones you see here. Practical women, too, weavers, midwives, expert markswomen with a rifle even. And yes, they carry such weapons with them, to protect themselves from the predators of the night."

Porter retreated behind the counter before saying, "They keep within range of Brother Thurgood at all times. Tonight that range includes your father. So all we have to do is transmit a warning. We see a wolf in sheep's clothing maybe, or a predator dressed like a man."

With a twist of his body, Traveler threw off the women, lunged across the countertop, and grabbed a fistful of Porter's T-shirt. "You're welcome to try me anytime you want, but my father is off limits."

Porter showed his teeth. "We are gaining strength day by day, Brother Traveler. One of our novices, Sister Smoot, proved herself just hours ago. She called upon sources in Salt Lake. And you know what they told her, that you were working for her father.

That an apostle of the devil has sent you among us. We won't tolerate outside interference, his or yours, *Mister* Traveler."

"Would you rather have me or the Danites in Fire Creek?" Traveler asked.

"All who oppose God's plan will be destroyed." Porter looked past Traveler and smiled.

Traveler tightened his grip on the T-shirt and turned his head at the same time. The ax handle, its blurred arc glimpsed out of the corner of his eye, caught him behind the knees. He collapsed totally, ripping away the front of Porter's T-shirt on the way down.

Through a haze of pain he saw the woman standing over him, the ax handle raised over her head, her gaze fixed in the direction of Orrin Porter. Her shining eyes looked out of place in such a lackluster, aging face.

"Man on first," Porter said. "Batter up, Liz."

Traveler wrapped his arms around his head and started to get up. The whistle of wood through air came an instant before the crack. The sound and sensation, remembered from football, told him a rib had broken. His side exploded with pain. Instinctively, his arms repositioned themselves to fend off another rib-shattering blow.

"A single to center," Porter shouted. "Two men on base. Hit us a home run."

A blow to Traveler's head stunned him. His vision faded. In the pain-lit darkness a woman said, "That's for my son, not you."

For a moment Traveler felt himself being dragged, then nothing at all.

The sun rose inside his head. When he tried to squint against the glare, one of his eyelids wouldn't shut.

"You need a doctor," someone said.

He reached for the eyelid but found someone else's hand.

"Goddammit, don't move. I'm checking your pupils."

Traveler recognized the voice, Marshal Peake's. The sun

moved, became a flashlight beam revolving like a searchlight looking for a marquee.

"Stay here," Peake said. "I'm going to get help."

The flashlight stayed behind, casting its beam on Traveler's shoe. The position of the shoe, of his legs, told him he was sitting up and leaning against something hard. He seemed to recognize the front of Shipler's before everything began to spin. The sudden dizziness made him sick. Just like football, he thought, a concussion, and keeled over.

TWENTY-ONE

Traveler smelled perfume. Hair brushed his face. The sweet smell intensified.

"Drink this," a man's reassuring voice said.

Hands held him, propped him up. The movement set off pain, like a lightning flash, inside his head. A glass rim touched his lips. He opened his mouth to say he wasn't Alice in Wonderland and swallowed a harsh liquid instead.

"You'll be fine," the man said, and Traveler never doubted him for a moment.

Traveler sighed. The pain eased, dizziness ebbed. Sleep took him before he could say thank you.

Sometime later he became conscious of a hand holding his. The scent of perfume was still with him. He opened his eyes expecting to see Ruth.

"Look at you," Martin said. "I leave you on your own and see what happens."

"You don't fool me." Traveler squeezed his father's hand.

"The soup's ready," Ruth called from close by.

Until then Traveler hadn't realized that he was downstairs in the sofa bed, Ruth's bed, filled with her scent.

Martin pulled his hand away and stood up when Ruth joined them from the kitchen, carrying a steaming mug.

"Are you up to drinking it yourself?" she said.

"I'm not hungry."

"Doctor's orders." Ruth sat on the edge of the bed and nodded at Martin. "Sit him up. We'll spoon-feed him if we have to."

Dizziness returned with the change in position. When he reached out to steady himself, his hand landed on Ruth's thigh.

"You have a concussion," she said, rearranging his hand.

"Don't feel sorry for him," Martin said. "He used to play football with concussions all the time."

"Homemade chicken soup." She thrust the mug at Traveler.

"How long have I been asleep?" he asked.

"It's two in the afternoon," she said. "Ed Peake carried you here about nine last night. Before he did, he got a radio message through to Jason Thurgood and your father."

Martin said, "We were in the middle of nowhere. It was pitch black and he still managed to get the two of us as far as an old mining road, where the marshal picked us up in his truck and drove us back into town. It was Thurgood who examined you last night. Don't you remember? He gave you something to make you sleep after he was certain your skull wasn't cracked."

"I remember the voice."

"Jason's not a man you can forget. Now tell me what happened at Shipler's, and why the hell you were dumb enough to go up against Orrin Porter without me backing you up?"

"I thought I could take him. I didn't count on the women and I didn't count on him being so well prepared," Traveler answered.

"What the hell do you two expect," Ruth interjected. Both men stared at her. "You drive into town and start asking questions. You're on Porter's turf now. One way or another this whole area belongs to him. The church wants nothing to do with this mess. It's afraid of being embarrassed by being reminded of its own early days when the real Orrin Porter Rockwell was at work.''

''You're right,'' Traveler said. ''I should have seen it coming. Only I was keeping my eye on Porter when one of his women hit me from behind with an ax handle.''

''Who?''

''I'd never seen her before.''

Martin looked at Ruth and grinned. ''That's the Traveler curse, you know. We have no luck with women.''

''Describe her,'' Ruth said.

Traveler's glimpse of her had been fleeting and filtered through a haze of pain.

''Older,'' he said. ''Forty, maybe forty-five.''

''Thank you very much,'' Ruth said.

''Not like the Shipler girls, anyway.''

''No name?'' Martin asked.

''Liz.''

''I thought so,'' Ruth said. ''The word's all over town. It's a big joke. Goliath brought down by a woman. It was Liz Smoot who hit you.''

Martin nodded. ''You see. That's the curse at work. Clobbered by the daughter of an apostle. Thank God we don't have any witnesses. Otherwise we might have to do something.''

Ruth sighed. ''When the marshal went looking for Liz Smoot, everybody at Shipler's told him that you'd tripped and lost your balance in the store, and that brought a shelf of canned goods down on your head. They said they'd swear to it in court if necessary. Now finish your soup.''

As soon as he'd complied, she took the empty mug from his hand and stood up. ''I'll fix you something solid now. Even a fallen Goliath has to keep up his strength.''

She hesitated in the doorway. ''I'll close the kitchen door so you two men can talk." She shook her head. "The curse of the Travelers indeed."

When the kitchen radio came on a moment later, Martin said, "What have you done with Bill and Charlie?"

"I was worried about covering your back, so I stashed them at a motel, out of harm's way."

"Do you think they'll stay put?"

"Probably not. You didn't either. You went off to see Thurgood on your own."

"Somebody had to talk to the messiah."

Traveler groaned. "All right. Tell me what he's like."

Martin paced for a moment before answering. "When you're with him, you seem to understand him perfectly. You look at him, you listen to him—it doesn't matter what he's saying—and you know he's special. But when you're away from him . . ." He gestured impatiently. "He eludes description somehow. Yet I've seen him at work, helping people. People with no money, no way of paying him, which he didn't ask for anyway."

Traveler's eyes were slightly out of focus, a complication of his concussion, but he could still see the glowing look on Martin's face.

"We talked about childhood mostly," Martin went on. "About growing up. And growing old, too, when the fires of ambition burn less brightly. And we talked about living with what we've made of ourselves over the years."

Traveler closed his eyes. "You liked him, didn't you?"

"I think he's a decent man. I think he's come here to help people without expecting profit."

"And his motives?"

"I know what he told me, that he had a debt to pay and a guilty conscience to keep quiet. We'd just gotten around to discussing it when the marshal radioed that you'd been hurt. So all I got was the fact that he worked for the Atomic Energy Commission at one time. He made it sound like a summer job. Apparently they armed him with a Geiger counter and put him up in a motel in St. George to monitor fallout during one of the bomb tests.''

''And?''

''Nothing. We never got around to any more.''

When Traveler opened his eyes, the room began to spin. He slipped a leg over the side of the bed to anchor himself. The spinning stopped, though the pain inside his head blossomed brightly like napalm.

''One thing's for sure,'' Martin went on. ''He's a man with a mission. Being with him, watching him set a broken leg, makes you . . . feel healed yourself, though you weren't even sick.''

''You sound like you're the one who got hit on the head.''

''When you meet him, you'll understand what I mean. People come to him because they believe in him. You can see that in their eyes.''

''They showed me the videotape again down at Shipler's,'' Traveler said. ''I saw the eyes of the woman who shot him. They were filled with hatred.''

''You'd have to be insane to shoot anyone, especially a man like Jason Thurgood.''

Traveler levered himself into sitting position. The movement intensified his pain. ''You sound like a true believer.''

Martin shrugged.

''Like someone who's found the messiah.''

''I asked him, you know. 'What do you say to people who are calling you the messiah?' In response to that, Jason Thurgood looked me in the face and then started laughing like hell. He kept it up until tears were streaming down his face. 'Only in Utah,' he said when he finally caught his breath.''

''I'm going to have to meet this man for myself.''

''To hell with that. When your client's daughter attacks you with an ax handle, I say the job isn't worth it. I say we invoke rule number one and leave this place as soon as possible. What kind of daughter did Josiah Ellsworth raise anyway?''

"She's a mother who'd do anything to save her son. Chinese herbs, acupuncture, Jason Thurgood, or Moroni's Children. And maybe she thought I'd come to stop her."

"Haven't we, in a way?"

Traveler squinted at his father, who suddenly seemed to be receding into the distance. "Nothing was said out loud, only an exchange of looks, but I'm positive that she attacked me on orders from Orrin Porter."

"If that's true, if he gets other people to do his dirty work, then he's more dangerous than we thought. Frankly I don't see his attraction to women."

Traveler collapsed back onto the pillow just as the kitchen door swung open and Ruth arrived, carrying a tray. "I've made custard pudding," she said. "That ought to go down casy. There's enough for two, by the way."

Martin shook his head. "I'm going down to Shipler's and talk to Orrin Porter myself."

Clenching his teeth, Traveler struggled up again. "It's too dangerous to go alone."

Ruth pushed him down and held him there. He tried to resist but didn't have the strength.

"You're forgetting something," Martin said. "As of now, I'm a friend of Jason Thurgood's. I'm under his personal protection. Besides, Thurgood himself invited me down to Shipler's this afternoon. They're showing home videos of his work."

133

TWENTY-TWO

Traveler managed the custard by himself, but only after Ruth threatened a force feeding. While he ate, he had a hard time focusing his eyes. Whenever he looked up from the bowl, her image blurred. When he managed to bring her into sharp definition, everything else in the room went hazy. She was wearing a man's shirt again, like the first time he'd seen her, and reminded him of a long-ago girlfriend.

Once the custard settled, she fed him another pill and soon her words were fading in and out, some sounding shouted, others whispered.

He licked his lips, tasted pudding residue, and something bitter. What kind of pill had he taken? he wondered and thought about asking, only he lacked the will.

After a time she began speaking. Her voice sounded distant and not quite discernible. Maybe yawning would clear his ears, but by now his jaw muscles felt slack and lifeless. His eyes wouldn't open either.

Sleep brought ax handles, masquerading as Louisville Slug-gers, swinging at his head. In self-defense, he managed to get one eye open far enough to see Ruth sitting in a chair beside the bed. An open book rested in her lap. Her head was bent over the pages; her lips moved as if she were reading to herself, only now he could hear the words.

"My husband and I were in the high school hiking club to-gether. That's when we first climbed Lost Peak. Seven thousand feet was quite an accomplishment, we thought at the time."

Her pause made Traveler wonder if he hadn't been carrying on a conversation with her and that a response was now expected of him. But his only memory was of swinging ax handles.

"After we were married," Ruth went on, "we used to hike up there to watch the bomb tests. Sometimes we'd camp overnight and it would be like the Fourth of July when the sky lit up. I guess we lit up, too, with all the radiation. Only we didn't know it at the time."

His eyelid closed of its own weight.

"That's where we got our cancer. The doctor thought so any-way, but he couldn't prove it, so the government ignored us like everybody else, even when my husband took sick."

You were lucky to have escaped, Traveler said, or thought he did, though the words sounded funny, as if they were inside his head and not spoken out loud. Or maybe there was an echo, her words bouncing around inside him.

"I didn't escape," she said.

He struggled to reopen his eyes, to confirm that she was actu-ally speaking, but the pain had come back, strong enough to blind him, yet impotent against her confession.

"Like half the women in this town, I had a mastectomy. We've become a society of one-breasted women, to be shunned, to be invisible to people because we make them uncomfortable, be-cause we remind them of their own vulnerability. They look at us and wonder what seeds of fallout they carry within themselves."

He must tell her to stop, he thought. He took a deep breath, steeling himself against the pain, and unclenched his teeth to speak. But in that instant, the realization hit him. She was speaking her thoughts, more to herself than to him. To acknowledge that he heard them would be a terrible intrusion on her privacy.

"They give you something to fit inside your bra," she went on. "A prosthesis, they call it. 'It's undetectable,' they tell you. 'No one will know.' But you know. You only feel safe with your clothes on. Never again can you undress for a man. To do so, to see the look on his face would be . . ." Her voice caught. "Thank God, my Frank had passed on by then. Thank God I didn't have to see the look in his eyes."

Traveler willed himself not to move, not to give away the fact that he was awake.

"Maybe one of the Children would take me on, an older woman to help with the cooking and the sewing. What would you say to that, Mr. Traveler? Does a woman need a man that badly?"

He stirred and shook his head despite the pain, anything to convince her that he was just now coming awake, that he couldn't have overhead her revelations.

"Are you feeling better?" she asked.

He opened his eyes but couldn't speak. The shaking of his head had started the room spinning. The sensation brought bile surging up his throat. He swallowed convulsively and panted.

"You look like you need another pill," she said, then helped him sit up, and held the glass to his lips so that he could wash down the painkiller.

"Try to sleep." She settled him back onto the pillow and wiped his brow with a damp cloth.

But he couldn't close his eyes without heightening the dizziness. When he reached out to steady himself, she caught his hand and held on tightly.

"Relax," she whispered.

He breathed deeply through his mouth, concentrating on the

rhythm of filling his lungs. Gradually, the pain ebbed and with it his vertigo. He hadn't felt this bad since the game against Dallas, when he'd played the last quarter with double vision.

When her words came again it was as if in a dream. "I heard Eula and Vyrle talking about Orrin Porter. They said he was hung like a . . . well, it doesn't matter what they said, because they knew I could overhear them. They probably thought it was funny because I don't have a man, and don't have a chance of getting one."

The floorboards creaked. Probably she'd left the room. He sighed, relieved that he was no longer a prisoner to her confidences. When he opened one eye to confirm that he was alone, he was looking at Ruth's back. She was standing at the window, staring out at Fillmore Avenue.

Without turning around she said, "How long were you awake before?"

He wet his lips. "I just woke up." Gingerly, he raised his head a few inches, waiting for the pain, for the dizziness. When nothing happened, he sat up. From there, he could see that her neck had flushed a bright red. He was trying to think of something to say when he remembered Bill and Charlie.

"Has my father come back from Shipler's?" he asked.

"He's come and gone, off to St. George to rescue your friends."

Ruth left the window to tuck the sheet around him. The room temperature had to be somewhere in the eighties, maybe even more.

Traveler sighed. "I think I'd better make a call to Salt Lake."

As she leaned over the bed to hand him the phone, Ruth's shirt billowed open at the throat. He stared despite himself. The plump swells of both breasts were clearly visible. Both looked normal and inviting.

"You are feeling better," she said, trying to make light of his stare, but color drained from her face.

"You're . . ." What the hell had he been about to say, You're a beautiful woman? It was true enough, but would she believe it? ". . . I'll call collect," he said for lack of anything better.

"Do you want me to get the number for you?"

Traveler looked down at the phone. By squinting tightly he could bring the buttons into focus.

"I'm fine."

"That's a relief." She left the room without another word, closing the kitchen door behind her. A moment later the outside screen door banged.

Traveler clenched his teeth and dialed the Joseph Smith Memorial Office Building from memory. Since he didn't have a direct number for Josiah Ellsworth, he went through a succession of assistants before the apostle finally came on the line.

"This is Josiah Ellsworth," he announced. "I hope you have good news for me, Mr. Traveler." He pronounced each word precisely. Some men did that when they'd been drinking. In Ellsworth's case, Traveler had the impression that the apostle expected his every word to be recorded for posterity. Or maybe the church recorded everything going through the Smith Building's switchboard.

Traveler said, "You lied to me."

"I'm an apostle of the church, Mr. Traveler. Maybe you didn't ask the right questions."

"You told me your daughter took your grandson here to Fire Creek for a cure."

"Correct."

"You didn't tell me she was a member of Moroni's Children."

"You've made a mistake," Ellsworth said. "My daughter would never forsake me or the church."

"She's in their power, you have my word for that."

"Explain yourself."

He did, recounting the details of the attack.

"Are you sure it was my Liz who hit you?"

"I'm told that's who it was, though I haven't confronted her."

"You have my authority, Mr. Traveler. Steal her away from those people."

"And your grandson?"

"Yes, him too."

"I don't do kidnapping."

"When I knew you were calling, Mr. Traveler, I asked Willis Tanner to be present. He's on the line with us. As you know he speaks for the prophet."

"Who speaks for you?" Traveler asked.

Ellsworth ignored the question. "Say hello, Willis."

"Mo, it's me."

"So?"

"You recognize my voice, don't you?"

"Yes, Willis."

"The prophet has his eye on you, Mo. If necessary, his spoken word is available."

Traveler thought that over. The last thing he wanted to do was talk to the head of the church. If a man like Elton Woolley asked for a favor, even a kidnapping, to say no would be unthinkable, at least if Moroni Traveler and Son wanted to continue operations in Utah.

"That won't be necessary," Traveler said.

"Then you'll do it," Tanner said. "You'll steal Sister Smoot and her boy away from those people?"

"I'll talk to her first, Willis. After that, we'll see."

"When?" Ellsworth asked.

"When my head stops ringing from the whack your daughter gave me with an ax handle."

"Do you need help?"

"When you came to me," Traveler said, "you wanted someone here in Fire Creek who didn't represent the church. You said the church couldn't afford to be linked with the likes of Moroni's Children."

"Have you seen Thurgood for yourself?" Ellsworth said.

"My father has."

"And?"

"Thurgood denies being the messiah."

"Are you satisfied with that?"

"I'll let you know when I've seen him for myself."

Traveler hung up, counted to one hundred silently, then called Willis Tanner's coded office number.

"Perfect timing, Mo," Tanner said the moment he picked up the receiver.

"Are you alone now?" Traveler asked.

"As much as anyone can be in my position."

"What have you got for me on the clinic?"

Traveler heard background noises and wondered if Tanner were starting or stopping his audio tape system.

"There now," Tanner said after a while, "that's better."

"Willis, I'm in bed with a concussion. My head aches, I'm seeing double half the time, so get to it."

"That's easy. Places like the Echo Canyon Clinic make me feel proud of this country. Who else but Americans would spend millions of dollars on medical research?"

"Stop with the press release, Willis, and tell me if it's connected with the Nuclear Regulatory Commission."

"At one time, with the old Atomic Energy Commission, maybe."

"I've been there. They all wear radiation badges, Willis. I have a cat carrier stamped RADIATION PROTOCOL."

"It's cancer research, Mo, what else?"

"The last I heard Down syndrome didn't respond to radiation."

"I've done my homework, Mo. I know you're working on a retarded boy who's missing from the clinic. Petey Biscari, isn't it?"

"If you know that, you know a hell of a lot more too."

"It's a government facility. Much of the work done there is classified. They're not going to tell me secrets just because I ask. Sure, I've heard the rumors. But I don't believe them."

"Okay, Willis, you're off the hook. I won't quote you."

Tanner sighed. "The word is they've been running tests on federal prisoners for years. You know the kind of thing. So many years off your sentence if you let them shoot you full of radium, or some damned thing. Volunteers only, Mo."

"And Petey?"

"They tell me that that part of the research is strictly separate, nothing to do with the rest of the clinic."

"Who tells you?" Traveler said.

"You know the church's position when it comes to national security. We back the government all the way."

"Like turning a blind eye when St. George became Fallout City."

"Now, Mo."

"One word from the prophet, and the government would have backed off aboveground bomb testing."

"We look at it this way. There are some risks worth taking. For the greater good, you understand. For argument's sake, let's say testing certain groups of people might save other lives someday. Wouldn't that be worth it?"

"Would you let them run their tests on you, Willis?"

"Ask yourself this, Mo. What if brain damage and retardation could be reversed medically? Would you support such research?

"Goddammit, Willis, what are they doing to people like Petey?"

"I don't know."

"Are you going to find out?"

"We never had this conversation, Moroni."

141

TWENTY-THREE

Traveler awoke from a nightmare bathed in sweat. He must have called out in his sleep, because he heard Ruth's footsteps rushing down the stairs. The kitchen light snapped on. She hurried into the living room, took one look at him and said, "You're soaking wet. I'll get a towel."

He swallowed dryly and looked around the room half expecting to see Josiah Ellsworth and his Danites out for blood atonement, but they'd been chased away by the light.

His headache was back, along with a stabbing sensation along the left side of his rib cage. His pain seemed to lessen as she wiped him with the towel and then handed him a dry pair of pajamas. She told him that she'd salvaged them from storage in the garage. They were with some of her husband's things which she'd been meaning to give away for a long time.

"Do you need help changing?" she asked.

"No."

"I think you're as shy as my husband."

Leaving him to struggle with the pajamas, she fetched a glass of water and a pill from the kitchen. After he took it, she touched his brow as if checking for fever, then took his hand and held it.

With a sigh, he closed his eyes. Suddenly, it was his mother's hand he felt, remembered from the nursing home after her stroke. He'd found her in the day room, kissed her forehead, then knelt beside her wheelchair to clasp her hand, trying desperately to communicate after so many years of silence between them. But she'd stared straight ahead, ignoring him and the roomful of patients and visitors.

"Mother," he whispered, "it's me, Moroni." Her only answer was to jerk her fingers from his grasp and hide them in her lap as if she wanted no further contact with him.

He'd spoken to her for a long time after that, at first reassuring her that she'd soon be home, then moving on to shared memories, picnics in Parley's Canyon, family outings at Liberty Park, ward dinners, anything he could think of.

Never once did she look at him.

Finally, when he could bear it no longer, he rose to leave. Only then did she raise her eyes to him. In them, he saw a look of derision.

It was the last time he'd seen her alive.

TWENTY-FOUR

A rooster crowed, in the backyard by the sound of it. Despite feeling rested and refreshed, Traveler opened his eyes tentatively, half expecting the pain to reassert itself, or maybe a flood of dizziness to overwhelm him.

Ruth was sleeping beside him, though outside the quilt. A ray of morning sun haloed her hair. Traveler immediately became conscious of the soft smell of her, and his own physical reaction to her presence.

As quietly as possible he slipped out of bed, hesitating momentarily to make certain his balance was stable, and tiptoed into the bathroom. While there, he washed his face and shaved, but that only emphasized the bruising on the side of his face, caused by a whack of the ax handle he'd been too far gone to even feel at the time.

With probing fingers he examined the rest of his bruises, which were no worse than any Monday morning following a football game. But that had been a decade ago. Time had been no kinder to his face than Liz Smoot's batting technique.

He looked, he thought, like a dog's lunch, but the pain was gone at least.

Creeping from the bathroom, he headed for the kitchen intending to make coffee. But one look at the clock told him the rooster must have been on daylight saving time.

Somehow, he managed to slip back into bed without waking Ruth. In his absence, she'd burrowed beneath the quilt, leaving only the top of her head and one ear showing. Smiling, he leaned close and kissed her.

She reached out to him without opening her eyes. When her lips touched his, he wondered if she was fully awake, if maybe she was remembering her husband. But she whispered ''Moroni'' into his mouth.

His tongue answered hers.

Breathlessly, she broke contact to say, ''Were you asleep yesterday when I spoke to you?''

''I'm sorry.''

She tried to turn away from him but he held her tight. ''Thousands of women have mastectomies, Ruth. That doesn't stop them from leading normal lives.''

''My dear, Moroni, this is Utah. Here only men lead normal lives.''

Rather than respond, he transferred his lips to her neck, still soft and warm from sleep. She raised her chin to accommodate him.

''About my breasts,'' she breathed into his ear.

''It doesn't make any difference,'' he murmured.

''I'm wearing my bra under my nightgown.''

''So you are,'' he said, exploring.

''If it's all right, I'd like to keep it on while we make love.''

He kissed her gently, moved by her trust, aroused by it too, more than he had been in years. "You're a desirable woman just the way you are."

Her hands slid over him. "I can feel your sincerity."

A few minutes later, in the excitement, the bra came off.

TWENTY-FIVE

By breakfast time, Traveler was ravenous.

"Time out for food," he told Ruth, who was beginning to stir in his arms again.

"And you said you could go all day."

"A cup of coffee at least, to bolster my strength."

Her hand latched on to him. "I promised your father I'd make you stay in bed all day."

When he began to respond again, she rolled away, laughing. "You know what they say about the way to a man's heart. How about hotcakes?"

"What would Martin say?"

"I'll tell him I served you in bed."

An hour later, showered and refreshed, Traveler asked for a guided tour. "Sightseeing only," he assured her. "No confrontations."

Holding hands, they ambled along First Street, renamed Nephite by Moroni's Children, for a couple of blocks before turning east on Brigham. After a block and a half, Brigham's pavement ran out, continuing as a steadily rising dirt lane that wound its way toward the foothills of the Furnace Mountains a mile away.

When they reached ground high enough to overlook the town, Ruth stopped and squeezed his fingers. "This is where I got my first kiss," she said.

He gave her another.

"I married him," she said.

He kissed her again.

Tears filled her eyes suddenly. "There were nights half the town came here to watch the bomb testing. We thought it was beautiful."

He wrapped his arms around her until she sighed.

"It's time you learned your way around, Moroni." She broke free of him to point toward the foothills. "You see where the road ends and the boulders begin? Behind them is Coffee Pot Springs, an old ghost town, dead since the mines closed. Jason Thurgood pitched his tent up there when he first arrived. For the view, he said at the time, though most of us figured he just wanted to be alone. Now his hospital's up there, an even bigger tent pitched in the middle of what used to be Main Street."

"Where do the Children live?"

"Just down the road. Most of them anyway. I'll show you, but only if you promise to be good."

"What's your definition of good."

"Getting me into bed one more time before your father gets back."

He kissed her. "That's the best offer I've ever had."

A block later, they passed the abandoned schoolhouse, a red-rock building two rooms wide with separate arched entrances for boys and girls. Four lines had been spray-painted on the side of the building, in the same red Day-Glo that defaced the sign on city hall.

A is for atom
B is for bomb
C is for cancer
D is for death

"That's how we teach the ABCs in downwind country," Ruth said, tears creeping down her cheeks.

In the next block, a neighborhood of dilapidated miners' shacks, she pointed to a new street sign. "By town proclamation, this is now Snelgrove Road. For a while there was talk of renaming Brigham Avenue too. They were going to call it Orrin Porter Drive, but even the Children were leery of messing with a street named after Brigham Young."

The shacks, blackened by time and the desert sun, had no front yards, no lawns, no flowers, only weeds that had been trampled into paths here and there. All would have looked derelict if it hadn't been for the vegetable gardens in the side yards and the large numbers of young children playing in the road.

"Maybe it's time you thought about leaving this town," Traveler said.

"On my own, maybe, but nobody's going to run me out."

They continued on another block, to Jaredite, the town's northern limit. There, next to the last house, Ruth introduced him to to a man who was hoeing a good-size vegetable garden, Earl Hillman. He tipped his hat but said nothing.

Once out of Hillman's earshot, she said, "Except for the kids, Earl's the only one of the Children I feel sorry for. I can't understand why he and Vonda ever joined them. Vonda's a strong woman, not the kind to put up with her husband taking more wives, which is the only damned reason I can figure for men signing on with these people. If she was going to shoot anybody, it should have been Horace Snelgrove. That man can't keep his pants zipped.''

"I know the feeling."

She punched him lightly on the arm. "Only one woman at a time for you."

By now they were paralleling Fire Creek, dry for the moment. Over the years, a deep channel had been cut into the red earth, its vertical sides reminding Traveler of a miniature Grand Canyon.

"We used to climb down and play hide and seek when I was a girl," Ruth said.

The gully looked to be twenty feet deep, its bottom strewn with jagged red boulders partially concealed by waist-high weeds. The closest house was a block away.

"This is the south end of Fire Creek," she said. "It floods during cloudbursts, though we haven't had one in years. At one time there was talk of turning the creek into a concrete storm drain. It was about then, though, that the downwind effect started to hit hard. Remember all those movie stars who started dying after making a picture in southern Utah? After that, nobody wanted to move here, not even miners. As for the rest of us, it was too late anyway."

"Don't talk like that."

Ruth went up on tiptoe to kiss him. "That's some pistol you've got in your pocket."

"Armed and dangerous, that's me."

She stepped back to look him in the face. "I want you, Moroni. Maybe even more than I ever wanted my husband, but I have no illusions about us. You'll be going back to Salt Lake soon enough and I'll still be here in Fire Creek waiting for the cancer to hit me again."

"There's nothing here for you anymore," he said.

"There's memories."

"We'll make new ones."

"I don't like the Children, I admit it. But this is still my home. I have friends here, people I've known all my life. Fewer and fewer all the time, I admit that too, but I don't want to live among strangers."

He started to respond but she silenced him with a touch of her hand to his lips. "Sometimes we women get together, our society of one-breasted women, and talk about the look in men's eyes."

She blinked, spilling tears onto her cheeks. "Dear God, I wish I were whole for you, Moroni."

"What do you see in my eyes?"

She laughed. "Lust."

He was about to kiss her again when he heard growls coming from the creekbed. Traveler leaned over the edge of the embankment. At first he saw nothing, only a narrow overgrown trail that ran along the creekbed.

Movement caught his eye. There, in the shade of the overhanging cottonwood, a small clearing had been trampled in the weeds. In it, two dogs were tugging at a body, whose blue checkered shirt was the same as Norm Shipler had been wearing the previous day. A flash of white, glimpsed through the weeds, could have been the man's leg cast.

"Get away," he shouted at the dogs.

They looked at him, wagged their tails, then went back to work.

"What's the best way down?" Traveler said.

She led the way upstream until they reached a steep path with crude steps gouged into the red soil. Traveler climbed down backward, as if descending a ladder, while Ruth waited. As soon as he reached the bottom, she followed.

The dogs, the size of German shepherds, looked up from their prize and snarled when Traveler and Ruth got within a few yards.

"They belonged to Mayor Gibbs," Ruth said. "They've been running wild ever since he went missing, though I think Norm Shipler's been feeding them."

Traveler drove them off with a barrage of rocks, making sure every one thrown was a near miss.

"You'd better stay back while I take a closer look," Traveler told Ruth.

Ruth shook her head. "I nursed my husband, watching him die. Nothing could be worse than that. Now, let's get this over with."

Shipler's hands and fingernails were ripped to pieces, but not from the dogs, Traveler thought. More likely he'd tried to claw his way up the side of the embankment. His scrambling could have dislodged the bloody rock that lay nearby, one that seemed to match the jagged hole in his forehead. Judging by the state of his shoes, the dogs had been tugging at his feet mostly. Probably trying to get him home.

"The poor man must have fallen in," Ruth said, looking up at the steep embankment and shuddering.

Being careful where he stepped, Traveler checked the immediate area but found nothing.

"You go get Marshal Peake," he said. "I'll stay here in case the dogs come back. Or something worse."

Ruth looked around warily. "You don't think it was an accident, do you?"

He shook his head. "His crutches should be here."

"Norm's not going anywhere, dogs or no dogs, so you're coming with me. I don't want to be alone right now."

She didn't want him to be here alone, either. He could tell that from her tone of voice. Against his better judgment, he left with her.

TWENTY-SIX

By the time Traveler and Ruth led Marshal Peake back to the location, Norm Shipler's crutches were resting on the lip of the creekbed, almost directly above the body. Ruth raised an eyebrow at Traveler but said nothing.

Peake said, "The last time I saw Norm he was drinking. He told me he'd lost his daughters and his faith, so what the hell difference did it make if he broke the Word of Wisdom."

"The crutches weren't here when we found him," Traveler said.

"You could have overlooked them in the excitement."

"We didn't," Ruth said.

Peake, standing on the brink staring down at the body, shook his head. "The fight went out of Norm when his daughters took up with Porter. You know that and so do I. He could have lost his balance. He could have jumped in, too."

"Bullshit," Traveler said. "The creek's not deep enough to guarantee suicide. I suggest you climb down there and look at his hands."

"I'll do that while you two stay here." Peake, who'd brought a rope and a tarp from his office, tied the rope to a small tree and lowered himself over the edge after tossing the tarp in ahead of him.

When he was kneeling beside the body, Traveler shouted, "If you ask me, he was trying to claw his way out when somebody dropped a rock on his head."

"Old Norm lived here all his life," Peake said. "He knew all he had to do was go upstream to find an easier way out. He must have panicked, that's all, tried to climb the bank, lost his balance and fell backward, cracking his skull open. Plain bad luck, that's all."

Traveler turned to Ruth. "Is he serious?"

"As big as Ed is, you can't expect him to go up against a man like Porter."

"It could be somebody else."

Ruth thought that over for a moment, then cupped her hands around her mouth and shouted at the marshal. "I swear, the crutches weren't here, Ed."

The marshal waved off further dialogue and went to work, spreading the tarp over Shipler's body and weighting down the edges with large rocks. After that, he grabbed the rope and climbed out of the ravine.

"I have to call the county sheriff anyway, even for a suicide," he said when he reached them. "But I don't think the forensic team will find a damned thing."

"And the crutches?" Traveler said.

"My guess is the only prints we'll find will be Norm's."

"What will that prove?"

Peake shrugged. "I'll tell the sheriff about the crutches. Whether he'll believe you or not will be up to him."

"Dammit, Ed," Ruth said, "are you going to let someone like Orrin Porter get away with this?"

Traveler took hold of her hand. "We could have been mistaken about the crutches, Marshal."

"What?" she said.

Traveler squeezed her hand, hard, and nodded at Peake, a barely perceptible signal. "Do you want us to make sure the dogs don't come back while you call the sheriff?"

"That's a good idea, but stay up here and out of the way."

"You can count on it."

"What the hell was that all about?" Ruth asked as soon as the marshal left.

"I'm thinking about what you said a few minutes ago. That this is your town and that you're not leaving. I won't always be around to protect you. Besides, we could have missed the crutches."

"You don't believe that."

"I don't see Orrin Porter having much of a motive. Shipler was already terrified of him and everybody else. The broken leg had seen to that."

Ruth shook her head. "I've known Norm Shipler all my life. I have to do something."

"Leave that to me," he said.

"What do you have in mind?"

Traveler took her hand and led her out of the sun and into the shade of a stunted tree. "I came here looking for the messiah," he said. "No, scratch that. I came here investigating a point of theology, or so I thought. Martin said there was more to it than met the eye, and he's probably right. As soon as the marshal gets back, I'm talking to Liz Smoot."

"You're a glutton for punishment, aren't you? That woman almost killed you once."

"This time I won't turn my back."

"She and her son have been staying at the Hillman house, though I hear Orrin Porter spends nights with her whenever he can tear himself away from Eula and Vyrle."

TWENTY-SEVEN

Martin was pacing out front by the time Traveler and Ruth got back to the house. Ruth took one look at him, at the two reservation Indians, and the tepee pitched on her front lawn, and murmured, "My God, I haven't changed the sheets or made our bed. Stall them for a few minutes." Without waiting for an answer, she made a beeline down the driveway and in the side door.

The Indians' tepee, though painted with animal totems, looked suspiciously like army surplus. Its flap opened and out crawled Bill, followed by Charlie, who immediately reclosed the flap, but not before smoke leaked out.

"We were discussing immortality before you arrived, Mo," Bill said by way of greeting. "Charles and I have big plans. Baptisms all across this state."

"And your friends?" Traveler said, nodding at the two Shivwits.

"Like us all, they seek enlightenment, Mo. With luck, they'll soon become our first live converts."

Traveler glared at his father.

"Don't blame me," Martin said. "They didn't stay put at the motel. I had to go all the way to the reservation to find Bill and Charlie. They wouldn't leave without their entourage."

Charlie, Traveler noticed, had a new medicine bag, a replacement for the one confiscated by the police in St. George. The Shivwits also wore bags around their necks, as did Bill.

"We had a vision," Bill said to counter Traveler's disapproving stare. "We came in answer to your need. Your father only supplied the means."

Traveler knelt beside the tepee, opened the flap, and took a deep breath. "I'd have visions, too, if I stayed in there long enough."

"It's true, Moroni," Bill said. "We've seen the way to help you."

With a wave of his arm, Charlie urged Traveler inside the tepee. "You must open your senses."

Traveler shook his head. "I have work to do."

The front door opened and Ruth came out to join them. After introductions, she suggested they move the tepee into the backyard where there was shade.

"We didn't want to do that without permission," Charlie told her.

"You have it. While you're taking care of that, I'll fix us all some lemonade."

"My father and I have someone to see first," Traveler said.

"I hope you know what you're doing," Ruth said and disappeared into the house.

"I see your luck with women has changed," Martin observed.

"It's too early to tell. In the meantime, we've got to see Liz Smoot, who's living with the Hillmans. She's also been sleeping with Orrin Porter when he's not otherwise occupied with the rest of his wives."

Martin groaned. "I don't want to think of the consequences if Josiah Ellsworth gets wind of that."

The Hillman house shimmered in the heat waves rising around it. Even Earl Hillman, on his knees in the vegetable garden, seemed to oscillate as he rose to greet Traveler and Martin. He wore a broad-brimmed straw hat and a red bandana around his neck to catch the sweat. Shouts of children playing came from behind the house, where a pair of woolly junipers provided shady hiding places.

Without preamble he said, "Being big-city people, you ought to know if those stories you see on TV are true, about the things they do to women in prison?"

"Not in a jail like St. George," Martin said. "Prison's another matter."

Hillman sighed so hard he sagged. "I only visited my Vonda once in jail, when I got her a lawyer. Brother Snelgrove says if I see her again, I'll be dead too as far as he and the Children are concerned. My Vonda's been excommunicated, you know, shunned for eternity, her name never to be spoken again."

He lowered his head. "Maybe I'm dead already, for even using her name to you. But a man can't break old habits just like that. Every day, every hour, I sin in my thoughts. I think of Vonda and pray for her."

Martin took the man's elbow, and led him into the shade under the eaves of the house. There, Hillman slumped against the weathered clapboard beneath a small window.

"Were you with her when she fired the shot?" Martin asked gently.

He nodded.

"Has she told you why she did it?"

Hillman closed his eyes, though they continued to move beneath his lids. "She said she had a debt to pay."

"What debt?"

His eyes shimmied behind the lids. " 'Payment,' she told me, 'to give the devil his due.' "

Traveler shook his head, rekindling pain from the blow he'd received. Talk of the devil, abetted by the haunted look in Hillman's eyes, reminded him just how dangerous cult country could be. A man Martin's age might not have survived the attack he'd endured. The thought kicked in enough adrenaline to start Traveler's hands shaking. He'd been a fool to involve his father in something so dangerous.

"I'm not crazy," Hillman continued. "I may sound it but . . . ." His eyes opened. "My Vonda is not the kind of woman to lie. When she told me that Jason Thurgood was the devil's man, I knew one thing for sure. That in her heart she believed it absolutely."

"And you?"

Hillman licked his lips. "It doesn't matter. She'll never be dead to me, no matter what. If I dared, I'd tell that to Brother Snelgrove and be done with it. But I can't. I shouldn't be talking to you. Norm Shipler tried it, and look what it got him."

"Why did you join the Children in the first place?" Traveler asked.

"Not for the extra wives, like some think. If I'd ever tried anything like that, Vonda would have killed me." He flinched at the sound of his own words. "I don't mean that. Vonda wouldn't hurt anybody. What happened with Jason, with the shooting, has to be some kind of mistake. No, I joined because I knew Fire Creek couldn't survive without the Children."

Traveler caught movement in the window above Hillman's head, a woman's face momentarily glimpsed. "Is that Liz Smoot inside?"

He nodded. "She hasn't set foot out of the house since your accident." He ducked his head. "Not an accident exactly, but you know what I mean."

"We'd like to see her," Traveler said.

"Brother Porter gave me the job of keeping an eye on her. He wouldn't want her having visitors unless he was present."

"I'll tell you what. Why don't I knock on the front door and see if she'll talk to me. You don't have to be involved."

Hillman, a good six inches shorter than Traveler, looked up and smiled. "You wouldn't be threatening me, would you?"

"Would that help?"

"It might if Porter ever asked me if I resisted."

"Consider yourself threatened."

"Then I'd better knock on the door for you, because she's under orders not to open it to anyone else."

TWENTY-EIGHT

Liz Smoot stood in the open doorway staring wide-eyed at Earl Hillman, who immediately thrust his hands into the air. "If Orrin asks you," he said, "I didn't have any choice. A man my age wouldn't stand a chance against someone as big as Moroni here."

Liz shifted her gaze to Traveler. "I didn't expect to see you without the sheriff. My father would like nothing better than to see me arrested for assault. So go ahead. Drag me back to Salt Lake in handcuffs." She thrust out her wrists.

Martin pushed Traveler aside to introduce himself. "It's a good thing my son has a hard head."

"My father sent you both, didn't he? Two men against one woman and a little boy."

Hillman retreated down the porch steps. "I'll be in my garden. Just shout if you need me."

Watching him hurry away, Liz shook her head. "That man walks around here in a daze most of the time. If it wasn't for me cooking, I don't think he'd remember to eat."

Traveler's first impression of her had been a fleeting one, interrupted by an ax handle. Seeing her now, he found it hard to believe that she'd been capable of such an attack. For a woman in her forties, she looked old-age frail, no more than a hundred and ten pounds, her shoulders hunched under the burden of her coarse homespun dress, cinched at the waist because it could have held two women her size. Her hair was knotted into a lifeless braid, and she wore no makeup to hide the deep lines around her eyes and mouth.

"You'd better get out of the sun," she said.

The living room was filled with rows of folding chairs all facing one direction.

"We use this room for prayer meetings," she told them, "so we'd better sit in the kitchen."

She led them down a narrow hallway and into a kitchen large enough to hold a pioneer trestle table and a dozen mismatched chairs. Once Traveler and Martin were seated, she fussed at the sink, staring out the open window into the backyard where the children had abandoned the junipers to jump rope, chanting, "One potato, two potato, three potato, four."

"Why are you living here?" Traveler asked.

"I had no choice," she said without turning around to face him. "You should understand that. I had to find a way to save my son."

Martin snorted. "What about my son?"

"I didn't have a choice there either."

Traveler remembered the way she'd looked to Orrin Porter for guidance, for approval, a moment before she swung the ax handle. "What hold does Orrin Porter have over you?"

She swung around and pointed a finger at him. "I know what people are saying about me and Orrin. Understand me. I'd do anything for my boy. I'd . . . I'd . . ."

He could see her searching for the right word. Finally, she closed her eyes and sighed hard, making her shoulders sag even more. "I'd fuck the devil himself if I had to."

Her eyes snapped open. "Don't look so shocked. Any mother would do the same."

"And is he the devil?" Martin asked quietly.

She smiled crookedly. "Orrin Porter was the one who took me to see Jason Thurgood. I knew then that it was a sign, that Jason had the power, and that Orrin was his guardian angel. That's right, not the devil. He was like the first Orrin Porter Rockwell, who protected God's first prophet."

"Are you saying that Thurgood is the new messiah?"

She nodded at Martin. "You've met him for yourself. What do you think, Mr. Traveler?"

"He's a good man, I'll admit that."

"Look into your heart," she said, "and you'll know, like I do, that the Lord's faith is being rekindled here in Fire Creek. I'm proud to be part of it and so is my son. If God wants me to be a wife to His messiah's guardian angel, so be it."

Martin shook his head. "I'd be willing to bet money that his real name isn't Orrin Porter."

"I know that. He told me so himself. He had a revelation. God told him to take the name, and the responsibility that went with it. God told him to become His avenging angel."

"Does your father know about your relationship with this man?" Traveler asked.

"I'm not yet a full member of Moroni's Children. My faith and commitment have yet to be fully tested."

Gingerly, Traveler fingered the lump on his head. "I'd say you've passed so far."

"I came here to see my son cured. I thought you were standing in the way of his salvation, Mr. Traveler. I couldn't allow that."

"Your father is worried about you."

"About his grandson, you mean. His namesake. His immortality." She placed her hands on the table as if to push herself away from further contact. "They say he's the White Prophet, though he's never admitted it, even to me. If it's true, if he commands the army of Danites, then I'm lost. Maybe we all are. Maybe the devil is too strong for us.''

Tears ran down her cheeks. "I have sworn a blood oath to protect the messiah. All of us have. Even if I have to fight my own father, I will honor that oath.''

Martin said, "When I asked Jason Thurgood if he was the messiah, he denied it.''

"My son is cured," Liz said. "Through Jason Thurgood, the Lord's hand has reached out and touched my boy. My Josiah is cured as surely as the Lord saved Jason from the bullet meant to kill him. You don't have to believe me. I'll show you the miracle myself.''

She stood and beckoned them to follow, out the kitchen door and into the rear yard where, despite the oppressive heat, the children were still jumping rope. Two girls were twirling the rope while the other four children took turns.

"Josiah," she called, "come here for a moment.''

The boy who was jumping rope broke free and came running across the yard. Traveler recognized him immediately, the rosy-cheeked seven-year-old in the healthy photograph, no longer resembling the boy with Hodgkin's disease.

"You see," Liz said.

Traveler took the photographs from his wallet and showed them to Martin.

Shaking his head, Martin said, "What kind of treatment did he get?''

"God's touch was all he needed." She knelt to hug the boy, who squirmed to duck a kiss. The moment she released him, he charged away to rejoin his friends. "All the rest you see here are Porter's children. Most of the houses on this block are his. Snelgrove and his wives have the next block down.''

"I thought this was the Hillman house," Traveler said.

"Because of who my father is, Orrin thought it best that I have a chaperon. It's a fair trade. I keep house for Earl now that his wife is away." Liz bit her lip. "Actually, she's dead to us. Poor Earl. We all pray for him constantly. To think that the woman he loved turned against God and tried to kill His anointed one. It's worse than murder, if you ask me. Vonda—" Her teeth snapped together. "It's best not to speak her name. We might give the devil an opening. A bishop's court was held after the shooting. Despite Earl's pleading, she was excommunicated, to be shunned for all eternity."

Liz hugged herself. "She will not be raised from the dead, and will burn in hell forever." A long sigh turned into a shudder. "But Earl loves her still. I can see it in his eyes. Sometimes I wonder if he won't turn his back on us, like I did with my father."

"Your father wants you to come home," Traveler said.

"Is that your job, to kidnap me away?"

"Kidnappers wouldn't be here talking."

"Tell my father I still love him, but I can't risk my son's life by leaving this place."

"What if he won't listen?"

"You'd better convince him, Mr. Traveler, and from now on leave me alone. Otherwise, I just might have to tell my father that the child I'm carrying is yours."

Traveler clenched his teeth. Martin was right. Follow rule number one and stay away from religion.

"He wouldn't believe you," Traveler said.

"Are you sure?"

Martin laid a restraining hand on Traveler. "Let's do like the lady says, and leave her alone."

Traveler stood up. "I think it's time I met this man Thurgood for myself."

Liz smiled as if she'd been waiting for him to say that. "I'll show you the way, then. I never miss one of his curing sessions if I can help it."

TWENTY-NINE

Liz Smoot, her son in hand, led Traveler and Martin across an old trestle bridge spanning Fire Creek and up the trail toward Coffee Pot Springs. The boy, who'd left his playmates willingly when he heard he was to visit Jason Thurgood, skipped along showing energy to spare despite the 100-degree heat of early afternoon. Though following a well-beaten track, red dust billowed at their every step.

"We're not allowed to bring vehicles up here," Liz said. "Jason says the fumes won't do his patients any good."

"It's the desert air," the boy said, sounding as if he'd memorized the comment.

Liz nodded. "He's heard Jason say that, that the desert air's practically a cure in itself."

Suddenly, she and the boy began to sing, swinging their arms to the rhythm.

> "Altho' in woods and tents we dwell,
> Shout, shout, O Camp of Israel!

No Gentile mobs on earth can bind
Our thoughts, or steal our peace of mind.''

Traveler knew the words. They dated from the 1847 Mormon exodus from Nauvoo, Illinois, after the murder of Joseph Smith. Martin joined in.

''We'd better live in tents and smoke
Than wear the cursed Gentile yoke.''

The path rose steadily until it passed between two massive sentinel-like boulders. Once beyond them, the land sloped downhill into a shallow valley a quarter of a mile away. In the middle of that valley stood Coffee Pot Springs, half a dozen weather-beaten buildings on the verge of collapse. The nearest structure, two stories of sun-blackened clapboard, still showed a faded sign: MINER'S HOTEL.

One match, Traveler thought, and the entire ghost town would be nothing but ashes.

On the hillside above the town, mine shafts, now abandoned and partially collapsed, had been sunk into the blood-red slope.

Jason Thurgood's tent, army khaki and smelling of Cosmoline, stood in the middle of what had once been Main Street. The tent's side flaps were rolled up and tied against the eave poles, probably for cross ventilation, though the desert seemed perfectly still. Two canvas-back camp chairs flanked the open door flap. A hand-held bell, an old school model by the looks of it, stood beside one of the chairs.

Jason Thurgood emerged from inside to greet them in the fiery sunlight. The intensity of his smile and dark eyes took Traveler totally by surprise. His presence, his magnetism hadn't shown on the videotape. There, if anything, he'd looked ill at ease.

Thurgood grabbed Traveler's hand and shook it as if intent on creating a bond. "You're looking better than the last time I saw you, Mr. Traveler. How's the head?"

"As hard as ever," Martin answered.

"And the rib?" Thurgood asked.

Traveler stretched. "As good as new, I guess, because I'd completely forgotten about it."

"Praise God," Liz said.

Grinning shyly, Thurgood scooped young Josiah into his arms and whirled in a tight circle until the boy squealed with delight. When Thurgood ran out of steam, the boy shouted, "More, more, Uncle Jason."

"Whew," Thurgood said, sucking air. "You're going to wear me out."

When the boy hugged him, Thurgood started spinning again.

"That's enough for now," Liz said as soon as Thurgood made a face pleading for help.

Martin made a face too, at Traveler, then mouthed silently, "I told you so." He glanced at Thurgood before adding, "A good man."

Traveler was nodding his agreement as Thurgood handed the boy to his mother and led them all inside the tent, where he insisted on checking Traveler's rib cage for himself. Traveler had been expecting a crowd, but the tent was deserted.

Thurgood washed his hands in a waiting basin before the examination. The basin sat on one end of a long wooden table; the other end was stacked with medical supplies. The only other furnishings were a row of wooden folding cots, army surplus judging by their drab khaki color.

"It must have been a sprain all along," Thurgood said finally, "not a break."

Traveler blinked, remembering the sound of cracking bone when Liz hit him.

"God heals in mysterious ways," Liz said.

"We are blessed," a man answered behind Traveler's back.

Traveler swung around to find himself facing Horace Snelgrove and Orrin Porter.

Snelgrove spread his hands. "You are blessed to be witnesses to a daily miracle."

"Is it that late already?" Thurgood said.

Snelgrove nodded.

"Afternoon sick call," Liz explained.

At a nod of assent from Thurgood, Porter left the tent and began ringing the bell.

"Thank God for volunteers," Thurgood said, looking at Traveler. "You're welcome to stay if you'd like. Maybe we'll have time to talk later."

Within a few minutes, people appeared, lining up outside the tent. The majority were women; most had children with them, either in their arms or at their side. When their numbers grew to more than twenty, Thurgood's volunteers—Snelgrove and Porter—performed triage by sorting them into groups, which were then moved inside the tent to form shorter lines facing the treatment table.

Traveler drew Martin aside. "There are too many people here for a community this size. They must be putting on a show for us."

"Look at Thurgood. If they are, he doesn't know about it."

Traveler had to agree. The man examined each patient carefully, scrubbing his hands meticulously in disinfectant after every encounter.

Liz joined them. "Jason never asks for pay. Those who have extra money donate what they can to replenish his stock of medicine. All the money I had in my own name, I have now given to him. I've asked my husband for more, also, but so far he has refused."

She pointed across the room to where her son stood close to

Jason Thurgood. "You've seen the miracle for yourself. Tell my father, and my husband too. Tell them we must donate to the cause."

"Has Thurgood asked you for money?"

"He refuses to touch it. At first, he wouldn't let the Children collect it, but we finally persuaded him that we needed donations to keep the clinic stocked. As you can see, we haven't been able to afford a proper examination table yet. We don't have electricity here either, so at night we must use kerosene lamps."

"Thurgood could move into town."

Liz shook her head but didn't elaborate.

"Did he use drugs on your son?"

"Drugs didn't work on Josiah. Nothing worked until he saw Jason."

Traveler watched those being treated, the way their faces changed when Thurgood touched them, the way their eyes shone. They had absolute trust in Jason Thurgood. That much was clear. Trust tempered by awe.

Two hours later, when everyone had been seen to, Thurgood waved Traveler and Martin over to the table where once again he was scrubbing fastidiously. "Mostly I see scratches and cuts, a few fevers, and an occasional broken bone." He displayed his dripping hands. "Preventing unnecessary infection is half the battle. The rest, the body does for itself."

"And in Josiah Smoot's case?" Traveler said.

"Look around you. Look what I have to work with. At best, I'm an old-fashioned country doctor. I don't do miracles. I don't lay on hands like the Mormons, or anyone else. Not in the traditional sense. Sometimes I hug my patients to comfort them, to reassure them that they're loved and respected."

"Is the boy cured?"

"There's always the possibility of spontaneous remission." He shrugged. "Who's to say what the mind can do?"

Traveler searched the man's face for guile but saw nothing but sincerity.

Thurgood chuckled. "You look like a doubting Thomas if I've ever seen one. I ought to know. I used to see the same look every morning when I shaved. Just another quack. That was before I came here. Here people believe in me. Of course, I've been lucky so far. I haven't lost anybody, except to the cancer that was here before me."

He smiled crookedly. "You start having a few young patients drop dead on you and the honeymoon ends pretty damned quickly."

Outside the tent, someone shouted, "Brother Thurgood, we have an emergency."

A woman, escorted by Snelgrove and Porter, carried a young boy into the tent. To Traveler, the boy looked to be five or six. His eyes were squeezed shut, his face pallid.

"He fell into the creekbed," the woman explained. "He can't move his head or walk."

"Put him on the table."

She looked terrified at the suggestion. "He's in awful pain."

"What's your name?" Thurgood asked the boy.

The boy whimpered.

"Tommy," his mother answered.

"Tommy," Thurgood said, "I can't make you better unless you help me. We're going to have to examine you on the table here."

Tommy opened his eyes.

"That's better," Thurgood said. "We'll be as gentle as we can."

The boy shrieked when they laid him out. His eyes went wide and unfocused when Thurgood touched him. His legs jerked as if by involuntary reflex.

"It's too pat," Traveler whispered into his father's ear.

171

Thurgood looked at the mother. "Hold Tommy's shoulders." The moment she complied, Thurgood nodded at Snelgrove and Porter, who combined to imprison the boy's wrists and ankles.

"Turn him on his side," Thurgood commanded.

The boy whimpered.

Thurgood ran his fingers along the boy's spine, up and down the length until finally he nodded to himself, stepped back a pace from the table, and took a deep breath. "Place him on his back, please, and keep holding his shoulders and legs."

When the boy was in position, Thurgood took another breath, stepped forward, and gently inserted his hand under the child's back, ignoring his cries. The boy's back arched slightly as if Thurgood were making a fist. Then, with a steady thrust, his free hand pushed down on the boy's sternum. There was a loud snap. Light came into the child's eyes. The pain was obviously gone.

Sighing with relief, Thurgood turned and smiled at Traveler. "With a spinal problem like this I would have preferred an X-ray, but I'm all there is around here."

"It's a miracle," his mother said, her voice rising.

"A miracle," Snelgrove repeated.

"Another miracle," someone picked up outside the tent.

Thurgood shook his head as if to dismiss any such suggestion. "When he fell he dislocated a vertebra. It was pressing against the spinal column."

He held a hand up to his face, saw that it was shaking, and thrust it into the back pocket of his jeans. Then, without a word, he pushed past Traveler and walked out of the tent.

By the time Traveler and Martin caught up with him—trailed by Orrin Porter—Thurgood was halfway up the hill behind town, sitting in front of an abandoned mine shaft. From there, Fire Creek was visible, and all of the valley beyond. Farther along the foothills, maybe two miles to the south, Traveler saw something glinting in the sun, possibly a vehicle.

Thurgood must have seen it too because he said, "The Children keep track of all strangers entering this area. They tell me that's a sheep camp you're looking at. A shepherd passing through, they say.''

"It must be Pete Biscari," Martin said. "I never thought he'd make it this far."

"You know the man?"

Martin nodded. "He's an old friend."

"There's an old mining road leading to his camp, or so they tell me. You can pick it up just beyond Ed Peake's gas station if you want to go visiting."

"Maybe we'll look in on him later."

"If you do," Thurgood said, "tell him he's tougher than I am, surviving alone in this kind of country."

"Oh, you're a survivor all right," Traveler said. "I saw the proof on a videotape, when Vonda Hillman put a gun against your chest and fired."

Thurgood shook his head. "I told them taking pictures wasn't a good idea. When I saw that camera, I knew that sooner or later it would bring someone like you."

"We'd like to believe in miracles," Martin said.

"I'm not a conjurer. I didn't come here seeking followers. I came here to find myself. What I found was people who needed me. I don't care what they believe in, or if they have one wife or twenty."

"Did she try to kill you or not?" Traveler said.

Thurgood raised his shirt, revealing a nasty-looking bruise in the center of his chest. "Why do we take great delight in killing one another in the name of God?"

Traveler thrust a finger against Thurgood's chest, at the same point where Vonda Hillman's gun had fired.

"Sacrilege!" Porter blurted.

Thurgood waved him away. "You see how it is, Mr. Traveler. The Children worry about me. They came to me before that meeting and insisted I wear a protective vest. As a result, Vonda's life is all but over. So from now on, this is all I wear.'' He tugged at his shirt. "If someone wants me dead let them come and get it over with.''

Traveler, who'd suspected a flak jacket, was drawn to the man just the same—to his charm and apparent sincerity. "I don't understand why a doctor would bury himself in a place like this.''

"Actually, my car broke down,'' Thurgood said. "I either had to walk or die of thirst. Fire Creek was the first place I came to.''

"Where were you heading at the time?'' Martin asked.

"I don't know exactly, so that lets me out as the messiah, I guess.'' He chuckled. "I don't look like one either, do I? Of course, you two don't look like father and son. Or even detectives.''

"The devil has many disguises,'' Porter said.

Thurgood shook his head. "I think the devil would be more discreet than these two. From what I hear about detectives, they specialize in digging up dirt. Is that your real job, to confront me with my sins?''

"That depends on how many you've committed,'' Traveler said.

"Your father and I talked about that the other night,'' Thurgood said. "It's easier in the dark, you know, confessing your past. You don't have to look people in the eyes.''

"We can turn our backs if you'd like.''

One corner of Thurgood's mouth twitched as if a smile had died prematurely. "That won't be necessary.''

Traveler said, "My father told me that you worked for the Atomic Energy Commission.''

"It wasn't as grand as you make it sound. I wasn't much more than an errand boy. Maybe not even that, more like part of a quota that had to be filled. They have to meet certain safety precautions, even if it is a sham. I had enough medical training to meet their criteria.''

"Was this connected with the Echo Canyon Clinic?''

174

Thurgood looked startled. "What makes you ask about place?"

Martin told him of their quest for Petey Biscari.

"My profession has a lot to answer for," Thurgood said finally. "Like everyone else, I've heard talk about the clinic over in Pioche for years, but as to the real truth of it I couldn't say."

"I'll settle for your best guess," Traveler said.

"The SPCA tried to get in there once because of rumors about experimenting on animals. They got arrested on the spot." He shook his head. "There's no society for the prevention of cruelty to people, so God knows what goes on. As doctors, we like to think our mission is healing and easing pain, but how often do you read about abuses in the newspaper? Too many times, if you ask me."

"Were you ever in the clinic yourself?" Martin asked.

"We're talking twenty years ago when I worked for the AEC. I don't know if that clinic came under their jurisdiction or not back then. If it did, or even if it is under the NRC now, I have the feeling anyone working for them would have to keep quiet about it, because of security clearances and things like that."

"Are you saying that you couldn't answer even if you wanted to?"

Thurgood shrugged. "Everybody has their own ground rules. Let's say I've done things I'm not proud of and leave it at that. My monitor job was the first of many things I'd like to forget." He sighed deeply. "I'd just gotten my bachelor's degree, and was about to go on to medical school when I saw the AEC advertising for what they called medical field researchers. It sounded like the perfect beginning to what I saw as my future career in pure research."

He craned his neck and stared up at the hot blue sky. "I should have known better when they said I'd get all the on-the-job training I'd need in a week."

He scooped up a handful of red soil and let it trickle between

ngers. "Do you know about the atomic bomb they called
ty Harry?"

Traveler and Martin nodded.

"There was another one later on, even worse. So damned bad it
not only didn't get nicknamed, it was hushed up completely. Just
another routine test, they said at the time. Hardly worth more than
a few paragraphs on the wire services. Only right after they let her
rip, the wind came up unexpectedly. Fallout was blowing all the
way to Chicago before the AEC scientists knew what the hell
they'd done.

"Me, I was in the Dixie Motel taking readings on my Geiger
counter. 'It's just a formality,' they told me. 'You probably won't
get any reading at all. The last time we had a man on the spot the
needle didn't even budge. He got paid for doing nothing!"

Thurgood snorted. "Thirty minutes after detonation they called
me and asked for a reading. 'It's off the goddamned scale,' I told
them. 'You're doing something wrong,' they said. 'Recalibrate
your equipment and we'll call you back.' I did what they told me,
double-checking myself with the field manual. God knows what
the roentgen count was that day, but that needle was all the way to
the top.

"When the range officer finally got around to calling me back
two hours later, the reading hadn't changed. By then I was scared
to death. 'We'd better alert the local police,' I told him. 'That isn't
your decision to make,' he said. Then he reminded me of the security documents I'd signed to get my clearance and the job. 'Any
unauthorized release of information could lead to a jail sentence,'
he said. He must have had my file in front of him, because I remember what he said next. 'Any breach in security on your part
and you'll never enter medical school.' "

"So what the hell did you do?" Martin asked.

"I kept supplying the bastards with readings for the next two
days. The needle on that counter stayed off the scale the entire
time. As for me, I took a shower every damned hour like clock-

work. The locals should have been doing the same thing too, only they were never warned. God knows how many of them died as a result.''

Thurgood wet his lips. ''I've been dreaming about it ever since. It's always the same. I'm standing under a shower, safe and cool, while everyone around me catches fire and burns to ash.''

''Jesus,'' Martin said.

''So you can see I'm anything but a messiah. I'm a coward. I should have run out into the streets and given the alarm.''

''They wouldn't have believed you,'' Traveler said. ''In those days, we trusted the government.''

Martin squinted at Thurgood. ''At least two people are dead at that clinic,'' Martin said. ''The Biscari boy, another young man named Whitlock, and God knows who else. I wouldn't want something like that on my conscience.''

Thurgood stared at Martin for a long time. Finally he nodded and said, ''I came here to help people. In the end that's all a man can do. Miracles are beyond me.''

Traveler dug the photograph of a sickly Josiah Smoot from his wallet. ''I'm no expert, but after seeing the boy for myself today, I'd say you have one miracle to your credit.''

''I wish I could believe that.''

THIRTY

By the time Traveler and Martin got back to Ruth's, the sun was beginning to lose its edge. The eastern slopes of the Furnace Mountains were cooling toward purple, while the air reddened as the first hint of an evening breeze began disturbing the dust.

Ruth met them at the door, holding a fluffy-looking Brigham in her arms.

"I gave him a bath," she said, "and guess what. Brigham's a she."

Martin rolled his eyes and groaned dramatically. "That's the Traveler curse at work. It's inevitable. Females, even cats, give us Travelers trouble."

She handed him the cat. "Your cat peed on my latest article."

"Ruth's a stringer for the Salt Lake paper," Traveler reminded Martin.

"It was my own fault. I ran out of old newspapers for the service porch, though God knows why she didn't use her litter box." Ruth grinned. "It's lucky I bought five extra copies down at

Shipler's. Because I wrote about Jason Thurgood, they ordered enough copies for everyone in town.''

"I wish you hadn't," Traveler said. "It might not be safe."

Ruth shrugged. "Don't worry. I practically called him a saint. Now, come on into the kitchen. A couple of apple pies just came out of the oven. You can read and eat at the same time.''

The story, buried in the newspaper's feature section, was accompanied by a grainy black-and-white photograph of Thurgood at work inside his tent, surrounded by supplicants. None were recognizable because their backs were turned. Only a passing mention was made of Moroni's Children. Instead, Ruth had concentrated on Thurgood's practice of medicine in a town that had been without a doctor for years. Young Josiah was not referred to by name, though his miraculous cure was detailed.

"Thank God you didn't quote anyone calling Thurgood the messiah," Martin said. "Otherwise, all hell might break loose."

Traveler put down his fork and said, "We just came from talking to Thurgood."

"So I heard down at Shipler's."

"Did you hear anything about a sheep camp?" Martin asked.

"Off the old mining road, south of town. That's the Children for you. They've been arrested for polygamy too many times not to check everything and everyone that comes into range."

"Can you tell us how to get there?"

"I'd better show you the way," she said.

Pete Biscari was sitting beside an open fire skinning a jackrabbit when they arrived. His flock, kept tightly packed by a working border collie, was grazing along the lee of a low hill. As before, the older collie, Janie, stood guard beside Biscari, eyeing the newcomers warily.

Biscari waved the carcass at Martin. "Jackrabbit stew just like you wanted."

"You should see this man shoot," Martin responded. "He can bring down a rabbit with a .22 rifle at a hundred yards."

Biscari shrugged as if to deny the compliment. "Let me get this one into the pot and I'll put on coffee."

"We'll have dessert first," Ruth said. She'd insisted on bringing along the second apple pie, wrapped in foil which in turn was protected by an extra copy of the day's newspaper. Biscari, who didn't have enough plates to go around, ate his slice of pie off the newsprint, smacking his lips between each bite.

"Women have a special touch when it comes to baking," he said. "I haven't tasted anything this good since my wife passed on."

"They told me of your loss," Ruth said. "I'm sorry."

Biscari appeared not to hear her.

"Have you had any luck?" Martin asked.

Biscari was staring at the remains of his pie. The dog at his side raised her head and whined anxiously as Biscari started to shake. At first the tremors seemed a trick of the flickering fire but soon became so apparent that Martin reached out in alarm.

"Pete, what's wrong?" he said.

"That's him," he replied, slowly crumpling the newspaper into his clenched fist. He raised his arm against the night sky and said, "I'd know that bastard anywhere. That's the man who was treating my boy. Dr. Jack Ottinger, from that damned clinic." Janie sat up and bared her teeth.

Gingerly, Martin stepped around the dog and pried the paper from his friend's hand. He smoothed it out and held it to the light. "That's Jason Thurgood. Three hours ago I was standing as close to him as I am to you, and that photo doesn't look anything like him."

"It's Ottinger," Biscari insisted. "The man who promised to take care of Petey."

For a moment, Traveler didn't believe it. The photograph, like most newspaper shots, was grainy and softly focused. If it hadn't been for the surroundings, the tent and Moroni's Children, Traveler wouldn't have recognized Jason Thurgood.

"Thurgood has blue eyes," Martin said.

Biscari nodded. "That's right."

"Dark brown hair. Maybe five-ten, a hundred and sixty pounds."

Again, Biscari nodded.

Martin spent the next ten minutes explaining the situation in Fire Creek, concentrating on the tent clinic that Thurgood had set up in the old ghost town.

The moment Martin finished, Biscari said, "I don't care if he's changed his name, he's still going to have to answer to me for what he's done."

Ruth started to say something, but Traveler restrained her with a shake of his head. He saw no reason to involve her, despite her authorship of the article.

"We're investigating Thurgood right now," Traveler said. "Let us do what we're paid for, and you stay away from him."

Instead of answering, Biscari paced around the fire, with Janie in step beside him. When he stopped beside Traveler he said, "You don't believe me, do you?"

"That won't stop me from doing my job," Traveler said. "We'll talk to him. We'll find out who he is."

"What would you do if some doctor had taken away your father?"

"One woman's already in jail for trying to kill Thurgood," Traveler said.

Biscari glared. "Could be she's got the same reason I do."

Martin said, "You have my promise, Pete. We'll drive into St. George first thing tomorrow and interview the woman. After that, we'll talk to Thurgood. If we connect him to your son, we'll come straight back here and tell you.''

"I can't stay here. There isn't enough grass for the sheep.''

"We'll find you.''

"You'd better hurry.''

THIRTY-ONE

The alarm went off half an hour before dawn. Traveler beat his father downstairs. Even so, Ruth had breakfast on the table by the time he reached the kitchen.

"I've been thinking about that clinic Mr. Biscari mentioned last night," she said as she poured a cup of Postum. "A bunch of us were treated there, you know, for our cancers. It took years, of course, and hundreds of letters to our congressman before they agreed to provide radiation treatment at government expense. By then, half those who'd applied were dead."

"Did you see anyone like Petey at the clinic?"

"Retarded, you mean?" She shook her head. "They had orderlies watching us all the time so we couldn't wander off. We never saw any other patients at all, though we did hear dogs howling once. The sound gave me the willies."

She hugged herself. "I tried to do an article on the clinic once, but no one would talk to me about anything except my own treatment. They said most of what was done there was secret government research, and I could get in trouble for even mentioning it in print.''

"How did they treat you otherwise?''

"I'm here, aren't I?''

Traveler kissed her. "That's one thing in their favor.''

She kissed him back and whispered, "I missed you in bed.''

Her tongue was rearranging his blood supply when a drum started up, in her backyard judging by the sound of it.

"Your friends in the tepee have been up all night,'' she said.

Traveler charged through the screen door and into the yard. The smell of marijuana carried all the way from the tepee, its smoke caught in the light spilling from the kitchen window. As soon as the door banged behind him, the tepee flap opened and Bill emerged.

"Come on in, Mo. Enlightenment awaits.''

"We've got enough trouble without you and Charlie getting arrested again.''

"We do God's work, Mo. And maybe yours.''

"You don't know what that is.''

"We've been talking to Miz Holcomb. She's worried about you.''

"What else did she say?''

"She cares for you. I can see that for myself.''

Traveler smiled. "Martin and I are leaving for St. George in a few minutes, so keep an eye on her for me.''

"Hear me out first, Mo. As you know, Charlie and I are on a mission to raise souls. When we told our Shivwits friends at the reservation, their shaman showed us a grave. An outsider buried on Indian land.''

"Who exactly?''

"We didn't ask. We didn't know anybody was missing.''

"The former mayor here in town for one. Now get your friends out here and I'll ask them myself.''

Bill shook his head. "It's their shaman you'll have to see, Mo, up on the reservation. We'll take you to him.''

Traveler thought that over. As much as he'd like to pin the ex-mayor's murder on someone like Orrin Porter, questioning Vonda Hillman came first. He and Martin owed Pete Biscari that much.

When Traveler and Martin reached the jail in St. George, the watch commander himself told them that Vonda Hillman was strictly off limits to everyone but her lawyer.

"We represent the apostle Josiah Ellsworth," Traveler said.

"Do you have proof?"

"In this state, who'd lie about something like that?"

"I can't take your word."

Traveler gave him Josiah Ellsworth's credit card, along with Willis Tanner's direct access number at the Joseph Smith Building in Salt Lake. The watch commander passed both on to the police chief, who made the call.

Five minutes later, Traveler and Martin were passed through metal detectors and into a conference room.

Vonda Hillman surprised them. They'd expected someone her husband's age, but she was at least twenty years younger. A good figure showed through the prison garb, though her hair was short and ragged enough to have been home-cut.

She sat facing them across a table, as directed by a female officer, who then left the room to watch them through a heavy glass window. As soon as the door closed behind the officer, Vonda said, "She told me you represent an apostle of the church."

Traveler nodded. "We're not here to investigate the charge against you."

"Our interest is in Jason Thurgood," Martin added.

She smiled. "You being here means the church must be after him. That does my heart good."

"We've been warned not to speak with you about your case or your motive," Traveler said.

"It's no secret. It's already been in the newspapers. I'll tell you what I told the judge at the arraignment. Jason Thurgood is an agent of the devil."

The perfect insanity plea, Traveler thought, especially if voices told her to do it. Preferably Jesus Christ himself. "Do you have proof?"

She laid a hand over her breast as if preparing to swear allegiance. "I was a member of the church all my life, following God's path. And then *he* came to tempt me away."

"How?"

She wet her lips but said nothing.

Martin said, "We've just come from Fire Creek. People there are calling Jason Thurgood a miracle worker. The messiah even."

Vonda shook her head. "The devil uses miracles to trick the faithful. 'Follow me,' he says. 'Follow my path.' Only it leads straight to hell."

"We attended a healing session," Martin said. "A young boy in terrible agony was cured."

She leaned forward against the table. "Are you telling me you witnessed a miracle?"

Martin shrugged. "You tell us."

"We can't speak further until I touch you, and that's against jail rules."

Traveler got up and knocked on the door. When the jailer opened it, he explained the situation.

"Handshakes only," she said, "while I'm in the room."

Timidly, Vonda rose to shake their hands. "I feel you both," she said and sat down again.

When Traveler and Martin also sat, the jailer left them alone.

"A woman has to be careful," Vonda said. "Sometimes the devil uses people without them knowing it. They become his advocates. Sometimes he makes people sick so he can cure them. Those are the devil's miracles and only an illusion."

Traveler watched her closely. More than age separated her

from Earl, her husband. She had an inner strength he lacked, convictions that she was willing to kill for.

Traveler said, "Are you saying that the Smoot boy's cure is only an illusion?"

Vonda nodded. "Liz and the boy stayed with us, you know, Earl and me. A sickly boy, on his way to dying. But not now. Now he burns bright with the devil's light."

"He's a child," Martin said, "an innocent. What does it matter who saves him?"

"A body without a soul belongs to Satan."

"What if Jason Thurgood is a better doctor than you think?"

"You haven't thought it through. Only the devil's creature could have survived my bullet. I put the gun right against him before I pulled the trigger."

Traveler looked her in the eye. "He was wearing a bulletproof vest."

She shook her head violently. "I know I'm right. That little boy was at death's door, then suddenly he was up and playing with the other children. That's when talk of the messiah started and when I joined the Children. Soon after, they started offering second wives to Earl, and I started wondering if I'd been tricked so they could spread their fornication. There was only one way to be sure. Lay hands on Jason Thurgood and know the truth once and for all. When I told Earl what I was going to do, he said, 'Woman, don't you believe your eyes when you've seen a miracle?' 'Feeling's believing,' I said. Earl laughed at me. 'Go ahead and do your devil test,' he said. 'See how far it gets you.' "

Martin groaned. "Are you telling us that you shook Thurgood's hand and felt nothing?"

"As good as," Vonda said. "When I held out my hand, he turned away from me, but not before I saw the look on his face. Squeamish, that's what he was."

"When did this happen?" Traveler asked.

"During one of his so-called tent sessions."

Traveler looked at his father, who nodded to show he was thinking the same thing. During curing sessions, Jason Thurgood was scrupulous when it came to his hands, constantly dipping them in disinfectant.

"Were his hands wet?" Martin said.

She nodded. "He could have wiped them, but he didn't. He just turned away. That's when I knew what had to be done."

Speaking softly, Traveler said, "He wouldn't shake hands with you because he wanted to keep them clean for his patients. They were wet with disinfectant."

Vonda stared.

"It's true," Martin said.

"Sweet Jesus, forgive me."

"One more thing," Traveler said. "Have you ever heard Jason Thurgood called by any other name?"

She shook her head.

"What about Ottinger?" Martin added.

She pushed back her chair and dropped to her knees. "His name is Jesus."

THIRTY-TWO

By pushing the Jeep hard enough to rip out a muffler, Traveler and Martin made it back to Fire Creek by noon. While Ruth made them a bag lunch, they rousted out Bill, Charlie, and the two Shivwits. Traveler's intent was to reach the reservation by midafternoon, examine a body that might be used against Orrin Porter, and be back in time for Jason Thurgood's evening sick call.

Ruth saw Traveler off with a kiss that had Martin speculating about grandchildren all the way to the burial ground. Once there, the scorching bleakness demanded silence as the two Indians and their tribal shaman led the way to a lonely rock-covered grave. The late afternoon sun still had fire enough to force Traveler to wrap his hands in handkerchiefs before removing the protective red rocks.

While Traveler worked, the Indians chanted, to take the curse off such desecration, Bill explained. The body wasn't deep, no more than a couple of feet. Even so, Traveler was sweating profusely by the time the last of the loose red dirt was removed.

He caught his breath. It wasn't the missing mayor; it was the body of a boy.

He immediately compared the dead face with a photograph of Petey Biscari, but the desert had already sucked out the juices. The boy in the photograph bore no resemblance to the shriveled mummy inside the jeans and tattered T-shirt.

"He looks like he starved to death," Bill said.

"It's the desert," Charlie said, "taking back life for itself."

The three Shivwits pulled Charlie aside to whisper in his ear. After a while he nodded and returned to the grave. "They say he didn't die of thirst. They say it wasn't the desert that took him either, but the light. The great pillars of light that the white man has been igniting in the desert for years."

"Jesus Christ," Traveler said, remembering the radiation badges at the Echo Canyon Clinic.

"Yeah," Martin added. "If it's radiation, it had to come from that damned clinic. Maybe Thurgood is Ottinger after all. Maybe the bastard's been experimenting on children."

Traveler turned to the Indians. "Where did you find the boy?"

Charlie conferred with the shaman before answering. "At a toxic dump site near the border. It butts up against the reservation."

"How could the boy have gotten that far in this desert?"

Charlie talked that over with the Shivwits. "They think he stowed away on a truck heading for the dump site. He could have jumped off and hid when the driver dumped his load."

"Why didn't they report it?" Martin asked.

Charlie spread his hands. "There was nothing they could do for the boy, and they didn't want to get into trouble for being that close to the site, which is a restricted area."

"The boy must be baptized immediately," Bill said.

Charlie plucked the photograph from Traveler's hand and held it out. "Look at him. He was touched at birth. The great spirit would never turn away from such a gentle soul. Our efforts aren't needed. I see it inside." Charlie tapped his forehead. "He has been raised already."

Open-mouthed, Bill stared at the usually laconic Charlie, who said, "Do your work, Moroni, so the boy can rest in peace."

Nodding, Traveler loosened the jeans, whose heavy denim had kept the boy's shorts from disintegrating. And there, sewn into the elastic band, was the name Petey Biscari.

THIRTY-THREE

Bill, Charlie, and the Shivwits Indians stayed behind to wait for the sheriff or the FBI, depending on who claimed jurisdiction, while Traveler and Martin drove back to Fire Creek. Once there, they headed directly for Coffee Pot Springs, ignoring the restrictions on vehicles in the vicinity of Jason Thurgood's tent clinic. They intended to confront Jason Thurgood without delay.

They parked fifty yards short of the red boulders that guarded the pass to the old ghost town. By the time they reached the stone sentinels, the sun was beginning to set. Yet even in the dying light, they could see the body sprawled in front of the tent, next to one of the camp chairs.

There wasn't another soul in sight. Even so, they drew their .45s as they descended the hill. When they reached the tent, the only sound was the flapping of canvas in the evening breeze.

Jason Thurgood lay on his back staring up at the sky with sightless eyes. There were two bullet holes in the center of his chest, exactly where Vonda Hillman had thrust her pistol. The red soil around his body was black with blood.

The bullet holes were small, Traveler thought as he glanced back at the crest of the hill.

Martin read the glance. "If you're thinking that's where the shots came from, I agree."

Around the body there were dozens of footprints—boots, sneakers, even bare feet.

"It looks like everybody in town's been here," Martin said, kneeling beside Thurgood and gently closing his eyes. "All the way back here, I kept telling myself there had to be some kind of mistake. Only a good man would come to a place like this to heal people."

"Maybe he was doing penance for a guilty conscience. Maybe he was too good to be true."

With a sigh, Martin rose to his feet before collapsing onto the camp chair.

"I'll be right back," Traveler said and jogged back the way they'd come.

At the crest of the hill, he began a sweeping search pattern with the beam of his flashlight. Just off the trail, out of the traffic flow, light glinted off a shell casing. It was from a .22, freshly fired judging by the smell of it. Next to it were the prints of the killers, where they had stood side by side.

Traveler hesitated for a moment, wondering if he should fetch his father to witness the find. Finally, he shook his head, pocketed the casing, and stepped on the prints on the way back to his father.

Martin met him halfway up the path. "Come on, Mo. We'd better get the marshal."

Martin didn't speak again until they parked in front of the marshal's office at city hall. "You know what I said to Thurgood that first time we met? 'Are you the messiah, like everybody says?' 'God, I hope not,' he answered. He laughed then, a crazy laugh thinking back on it now. 'If Christ came again,' he told me, 'they'd have to kill him to keep his mouth shut. No one wants to hear that stuff about the eye of a needle. People want to think that the more money they make, the more God loves them.' ''

Martin got out of the Jeep and slammed the door. "I don't care if he did walk away from that clinic. It doesn't change the fact that he did something to Petey Biscari and the Whitlock boy that drove them into the desert. God knows how long they suffered out there. If you ask me, he got off easy."

THIRTY-FOUR

By the time they'd driven Marshal Peake back to the tent, there was no body. Even the blood-soaked soil where Thurgood had lain had been scooped out and carried away, leaving a body-size depression.

"Shit," Peake said. "That's cults for you. They clean up their own messes. Without evidence, we're up shit creek."

"Call the county sheriff," Martin said. "Dump it in his lap."

Peake adjusted the wick on one of the two hissing Coleman lanterns he'd brought along. "I'm willing to take your word that Jason Thurgood was killed here, but the sheriff won't. And you know what happens if I bring in more outsiders. Nobody talks to them. The Children close ranks and so do most of the locals."

"We're outsiders," Martin said, "and people have been talking to us."

"That's only because they know you're checking up on the Smoot woman. Nobody wants to rile a man like Josiah Ellsworth."

"You can't ignore another murder," Traveler said.

Peake removed his cowboy hat and pretended to study its sweat band. "There are a lot of people around town who'll say that the murders are your doing. Your way of stirring up trouble. Take Norm Shipler, for instance. What with his broken leg and the fact that he'd been drinking, according to witnesses down at the Escalante, chances are he fell in the creek and killed himself. Maybe he didn't even give a shit by then, and who could blame him considering the way his daughters had been acting up."

"What witnesses?" Traveler asked.

"Most of them are Moroni's Children, so what? They're still willing to swear to it. As long as they do that, Norm's death comes up an accident. As for Jason Thurgood, I have only your word that he's dead. For all I know, you two have got murder on the brain."

"I thought you believed us," Traveler said.

He shrugged. "I'd be a fool not to keep my options open."

"As long as you're doing that," Martin said, "let's up the count and make it three murders."

In detail, Martin recounted the opening of Petey Biscari's grave on the Indian reservation. As he was speaking, two women, both carrying flashlights, lined up outside the entrance to the tent, apparently expecting a late evening sick call. Their faces shone in the white lantern light.

After a long silence, Peake spoke softly. "I don't like the thought of a young boy dying like that, but as far as I can see it has nothing to do with Fire Creek."

"His father has identified the boy's doctor as Jason Thurgood," Traveler said, leaving out the Ottinger name change to keep things simple. "Petey ran away from the Echo Canyon Clinic. Somehow he made it far enough for the Indians to find him."

"Shit," Peake said, cramming his hat on his head. "You're talking about that government research center over by Pioche, aren't you?"

Traveler nodded.

"They may be calling it a clinic now, but there was a time when it was an animal research lab for the atomic bomb testing. They used to stake animals out in cages, starting at ground zero and working out from there, to see where survival and cancer took over. Not many people know about it, but back in '57 some scientists came to my dad's ranch asking to rent a strip of land. That was just before the big shot they call Dirty Harry. Anyway, they paid him good money to cage the animals along our fence line. Of course, Dad had to sign a paper saying he'd keep it to himself.

"They told him he'd be perfectly safe and so would the animals, dogs, cats, and the like. Our place was miles away from ground zero, they said, across the Nevada border. Well, you'd have to know my Dad to understand, but he took a fancy to one of them dogs they'd penned up. Hell, he went from cage to cage refilling their water bowls, which none of them scientists had thought to do. Anyway, when they came to collect their cages after Dirty Harry lit up half the state, they were missing a dog. My dad told them it must have got loose on its own.

"That dog took sick and died soon after. He was caged up only a mile from our ranch." Peake sighed. "A mile can mean a lot. It took my father another ten years before the cancer got him. I was up in Salt Lake at the time of the shot, taking law enforcement classes at the university. Otherwise, I'd be dead too."

The marshal smiled grimly. "If Jason Thurgood worked at that clinic, I say to hell with him."

"Fine," Martin said. "That still leaves us with two murders."

Outside the tent, the two women had been joined by half a dozen others.

"I'd like nothing better than to pin a murder on those scientists, but they're out of my jurisdiction and so is the Indian reservation. You never know, though. I might pick up some gossip sitting around city hall, or pumping gas. Take Norm Shipler's girls, for instance. To look at them, you wouldn't think they had any sense at all. But their father's death shook them, that's for sure. Ever since they saw his body, Eula and Vyrle have been telling me things.''

Peake adjusted his hat. ''Maybe I'll tell them a few things of my own. Who knows? They might believe me. Maybe Orrin will visit their beds one time too many.''

He chuckled. ''It kind of gives you the willies, doesn't it, thinking how vulnerable a man is during sex, especially if it's a threesome. Two women against one man. Maybe he falls asleep afterward and is just lying there, naked and exposed. One swipe of a razor and he's singing soprano. Now that's what I call blood atonement at its best.''

By now, a large crowd had materialized outside the tent, mostly women and children, though Snelgrove and Porter stood at the head of the line, carrying lanterns of their own.

An angry shout went up when the marshal started to leave with Traveler and Martin.

As if on cue, Snelgrove raised a hand to quiet his people. ''Where is our messiah?'' he demanded. ''He must not be bothered by the likes of you.''

''I haven't seen him,'' Peake said.

Snelgrove waved Porter inside the tent. Traveler had the feeling that it was a gesture only, a way for Snelgrove to show his power over his people, and over anyone who dared confront them.

A moment later Porter emerged, raised his lantern above his head and announced, ''Our messiah has been taken from us.''

Traveler stared at the faces confronting him. He saw confusion, maybe even hatred, but no immediate threat of violence. Even so, frankness was always a risk, but one he decided to take. ''Jason Thurgood has been shot.'' Traveler poked his chest to show the spot.

''Where is his body?'' Snelgrove demanded.

''It's disappeared,'' Peake answered.

Snelgrove shook his head. "It's as I feared. The messiah has been taken from us and crucified again."

"He was shot," Traveler repeated.

"It makes no difference," Snelgrove said. "The wounds of Christ are upon him."

A woman wailed. Another joined her, their cries instantly contagious to the children.

At a nod from Snelgrove, Porter thrust two fingers into his mouth and whistled shrilly. When calm was restored, Snelgrove signaled his followers to go down on their knees in prayer.

" 'O how great the goodness of our God,' " he said, " 'who prepareth a way for our escape from the grasp of this awful monster; yea, that monster, death and hell.' "

"I have become Elijah," Porter added. "He who will announce the messiah's coming."

Martin whispered, "Do you remember your Sunday school?"

Traveler nodded. According to the Hebrew Bible, the prophet Elijah would walk the earth again when the time came to proclaim a messiah.

"He is close at hand," Porter went on, "but must be protected from the infidels." He pointed a finger at Traveler.

For a moment, Traveler thought he had misread the Children's mood, that an eruption of violence was a possibility after all.

Then suddenly Snelgrove beckoned his people to their feet and led them into the darkness.

"Come on," Martin said, grabbing Traveler's arm. "We'd better find Pete Biscari and tell him about his son, not that he wasn't expecting it."

THIRTY-FIVE

Using Pete Biscari's campfire as a beacon, Traveler managed to get the Jeep within walking distance without breaking an axle. As usual, Biscari was sitting in front of the fire with the border collie at his side.

"I was hoping you'd come," he said as soon as they joined him. He nodded at the heavy iron pot hanging over the fire. "Fresh jackrabbit stew just the way you like it, Martin. It ought to be ready anytime now."

"We can't stay, Pete. Mo's ladyfriend is waiting dinner for us."

Biscari sighed so deeply that his shoulders rose and fell. "If you didn't drive all the way out here for my cooking, it must be bad news."

Martin ducked his head, unable to look Biscari in the eye. "Pete, we've been friends for a long time. I wish that I weren't the one to have to tell you. We've been up on the Shivwits reservation. They found a body."

"Petey?"

Traveler handed him the name tag that had been sewn into the boy's underwear.

"How did he die?"

"It's hard to know for sure," Martin answered.

"I can read your face. Tell me."

"The Indians say the light killed him," Traveler said. "From the bomb testing."

"I was right, then. Ottinger and that damn clinic are to blame." Biscari tucked away the name tag. "That reservation's on federal land. They'll cover it up, like everything else they do at that clinic."

"Thurgood is dead," Traveler said. "Shot."

"You mean Ottinger," Biscari replied, giving Traveler a level gaze. "Shooting is a better death than my boy got. They say radiation makes you waste away. They say it takes a long time, not like a bullet. But now at least Petey will be coming home to rest beside his mother."

"Do you want us to drive you to the reservation?" Martin said.

"I can't leave the sheep. Petey would understand that."

"We'll make the arrangements, then."

Biscari nodded and shook their hands. "Martin," he said, "you have a fine son. It gives me peace to know that you have such a son." Then he turned and walked away from the firelight, the dog beside him. They left side-by-side footprints just the way they'd done on the trail above Coffee Pot Springs.

For a moment, Traveler was tempted to call Biscari back and confront him. But the look on Martin's face made that impossible.

THIRTY-SIX

Traveler didn't remember getting into the Jeep and driving back through town; he didn't realize that Martin had parked in front of Ruth's until his father tapped him on the shoulder.

"You know what I'm thinking?" Martin said. "That maybe Vonda was right after all. That maybe it was the devil she was trying to kill."

"Someone should end up in hell, that's for sure."

They climbed out of the Jeep, and went inside, where Ruth greeted them with the cat in her arms.

"Brigham was getting lonely in the service porch," she said.

Martin held out his arms. Brigham went wide-eyed during the exchange but calmed when Martin settled onto the sofa and began stroking her gently. After a while, the cat closed her eyes and began to purr.

"Sure," Martin said, "women love soft-talking you in the beginning."

Ruth latched on to Traveler's hand. "You look terrible."

"Someone shot Jason Thurgood. Only this time he wasn't wearing a bulletproof vest."

"And now the body's disappeared," Martin added, "and Snelgrove and his friends are claiming crucifixion and resurrection, while Marshal Peake seems to be waiting for divine intervention."

Ruth put her arms around Traveler. "I don't want you doing anything dangerous."

Traveler led Ruth to the sofa, sat her beside Martin, and knelt in front of her.

"We found Biscari's son buried on the reservation," he said. "The Indians say radiation killed him. Looking at him, I'd have to agree."

"You see why I renamed this town Downwind. We're all dead, murdered legally by our own government. It would have been better if they'd put a gun to our heads." She sighed deeply. "That's why I became a stringer, to write about what's been going on downwind. Only, the editors like stories with happy endings."

After a late dinner, Traveler and Ruth sat side by side on the front lawn watching the night sky.

"Sometimes I wish you hadn't come here," she said after a long silence. "Maybe none of this would have happened, then. Maybe Norm Shipler and Jason would still be alive."

"And the boy?"

She leaned against him. "Because of you, Fire Creek will never be the same. Neither will I." She kissed his hand, then held it to her breast. "You've made me very happy." She rose up on her knees to kiss his mouth.

"Come to Salt Lake with me," he breathed.

"I don't want you with me when the cancer comes again."

He wrapped his arms around her. "You don't know that it will."

"Moroni . . ."

His lips closed over hers. She tried to say something more but her words were lost inside him.

Suddenly, she broke away from him, sobbing. "Dear God. They're at it again."

She pointed at a glow in the western sky. As Traveler watched, the light grew, mushrooming.

"How many tests before they kill us all?" Ruth said.

"That's no bomb. It's too close."

The screen door banged as Martin came out onto the stoop. "What the hell is that?"

Traveler got to his feet, pulling Ruth up after him.

She stared at the fiery sky and rubbed her arms. "It must be Coffee Pot Springs."

"We'd better take a look," Martin said.

"I'm going too," she said, and drove the Jeep Cherokee while Traveler and Martin checked their .45s. Rather than risk driving into a pothole in the dark, they abandoned the Jeep a quarter of a mile short of the boulders and hiked the rest of the way, using flashlights from the emergency kit Martin kept in the back.

"If anyone's guarding the pass, they'll see us coming," Ruth said.

Martin's answer was to jack a shell into the chamber of his pistol.

The wind shifted, blowing smoke in their faces.

"Christ," Martin said. "Do you smell it?"

"Like a barbecue," she said.

"A human barbecue."

Traveler stopped, holding her back. "You'd better go back to the Jeep."

She shook free of his grasp. "Come on. Let's get it over with."

By the time they crested the hill, every building in Coffee Pot Springs was burning. Even Thurgood's tent was on fire, though it was burning more brightly than canvas would account for, Traveler thought. Around it, their faces radiant in reflected light, stood Horace Snelgrove, Orrin Porter, and Earl Hillman.

By the time Traveler reached the tent, the smell of gasoline was overpowering.

" 'And the Lord went before them by day in a pillar of cloud,' " Snelgrove shouted, " 'and by night in a pillar of fire.' The messiah has come and gone, and we are his apostles.''

THIRTY-SEVEN

I would have done the same in their place,'' Martin said once he and Traveler were settled at Ruth's kitchen table, watching her pour a saucer of warm milk for Brigham. "You steal the body and burn it. Once that's done, who's to say Jason Thurgood hasn't risen from the grave like Christ? That's the way to create a religion.''

Ruth banged her saucepan on the sink. "You wouldn't hear a woman talking like that. Jason Thurgood was shot. Moroni's Children have destroyed evidence. That's a crime, pure and simple. They should be arrested.''

"We didn't catch them striking the match,'' Traveler said.

"And we can't prove it was Thurgood they were cremating,'' Martin added. "Or who killed him for that matter, thank God.''

Ruth glared. "Why thank God? And why would they burn a man's body if they weren't responsible for his death?''

"For the sake of argument,'' Traveler said, "let's say they didn't kill him but only found the body. Like Martin said, it's an opportunity in the making. If they compare him with Christ long enough, somebody might start believing it.''

"Thank God we weren't hired to investigate a homicide," Martin added.

Ruth sat beside Traveler. "I say thank God too, then. You told me yourself that you were hired to find out if Jason Thurgood was the messiah. Now that he's dead, there's nothing more you can do. Leave it at that. It's safer.''

Sure, Traveler thought. All he had to do was call Josiah Ellsworth and give him the bad news. *Thurgood has gone up in flames,* he'd say. *Not quite a resurrection from Joseph of Arimathaea's sepulcher, but the stuff of legend nevertheless. A legend being spread by the likes of Horace Snelgrove and Orrin Porter, now calling themselves apostles.*

The apostle, Josiah Ellsworth, returned Traveler's call shortly after midnight.

"I've heard from my daughter," he said without preamble. "She wants to come home now that Jason Thurgood is dead.''

"Did she tell you how he died?" Traveler asked. Martin was standing beside him, listening in.

"I won't be preached to," Ellsworth said, "by relatives or employees. And I won't tolerate blasphemy either. Just get her and bring her home.''

"You hired me to investigate a messiah.''

"My Liz says she's in danger. That takes precedent.''

"Even Moroni's Children have more sense than to touch your daughter.''

"She's made some kind of foolish liaison with a man calling himself Orrin Porter, and she's afraid what he might do when she tries to leave. You do this for me, Mr. Traveler, and I'll consider it a personal favor, one to be repaid.''

"We'll have to wait for daylight," Traveler said.

"I'm not willing to take that kind of chance," Ellsworth replied. "By morning I could have my own people in place."

Martin snatched the phone and clamped his hand over the receiver and whispered, "Better us than the Danites, Mo."

Nodding, Traveler took back the phone and told the apostle, "We'll do what we can."

"I've arranged to have my grandson and my daughter examined at the BYU medical center," Ellsworth responded. "How soon can you get them there?"

"About dawn if we're lucky."

"I'll be there," Ellsworth said and hung up.

Traveler woke up Ruth. Brigham, who was sleeping beside her, mewed in protest. As soon as she sat up, Ruth grabbed a fistful of tissue and started sneezing.

"You should keep Brigham in the garage," Traveler said. "You must be allergic."

"We were both lonely."

Traveler kissed her between sneezes. "We've been ordered to grab Liz Smoot and her son and take them out of here tonight. I want you to come with us."

"What do you mean, ordered?"

Traveler explained the situation.

"This is my home," Ruth said quietly. "There's nothing for me in Salt Lake."

"There's me."

Ruth shook her head slowly. "The radiation's still with us here. I guess it always will be. I can't ask you to stay."

He stared into her eyes and knew he'd been expecting such a rejection all along. He wondered if that's why he'd been attracted to her in the first place, because permanent commitment was never an option.

Martin's advice, given when Traveler was twelve, came back to him. It had come at the insistence of Kary, who said it was time her son knew the facts of life and that it was a father's duty to provide them.

Martin had taken Traveler into his room then, sat him on the bed, and winked because they'd already had such a discussion, complete with pictures from a medical book. This time, however, Martin rolled his eyes at the bedroom door where Kary was listening and said loud enough for her to hear, "About women, Mo, have nothing to do with them."

Thinking back on it, Traveler realized that Martin hadn't been joking.

He smiled at Ruth and heard a voice say, "Marry me." He realized it was his own.

She shook her head. "I can't have children."

"It doesn't matter."

She handed him the cat. "Goodbye, Moroni. Take Brigham with you. I don't want the downwind getting her too."

He kissed Ruth gently, unsure of what he was feeling, and left without another word.

THIRTY-EIGHT

Traveler parked the Jeep across the street from the Hillman house, switched off the engine, and waited. Brigham and her supplies were stowed in the backseat.

Finally, Traveler rolled down his window. There was a faint smell of smoke in the air, as if Jason Thurgood might still be smoldering. Traveler held his breath and listened. There was no sound. The only light came from a yellow porch bulb three houses away.

Five minutes passed before Martin said, "If they'd heard us coming, they'd have reacted by now. Let's get it over with."

They circled the house slowly, stopping to listen every few yards. At each step, dry weeds crackled underfoot. When they finished their tour without triggering a response, Traveler knocked on the front door, softly at first, then loud enough to be heard throughout the house, while Martin, his .45 drawn, covered their backs.

Traveler tried the door, found it locked, and kept applying pressure until the flimsy wooden frame gave way. His flashlight beam showed an empty living room and part of the kitchen beyond. The door to the inside hallway was closed.

They stepped inside, closing the ruined front door behind them. At that moment a light came on in the kitchen. Traveler turned toward it just as the hall door opened behind him. Another light snapped on, revealing Orrin Porter holding Liz Smoot in front of him, her fragile neck caught in the crook of his arm. His free hand held an ax handle. Behind him were Snelgrove and Hillman, holding the boy between them; they too carried ax handles.

Porter tightened his grip until Liz gasped. The sound brought a smile to his lips.

Traveler felt a surge of adrenaline, the same rush he'd felt at the opening kickoff of each football game. *Psych yourself,* his coach had preached. *Play crazy. It's the only way to survive.*

Traveler's hands trembled, but he spoke quietly, enunciating each word like a drunk intent on passing a sobriety test. "We've come to take Mrs. Smoot and her son home."

"Kidnapping a man's wife is a crime," Porter responded. "Isn't that right, my love." He flexed his arm to make her head nod.

"If we don't take her, the Danites will."

"Fairy tales and bogeymen."

"You've taken the name of one of those bogeymen," Traveler reminded him.

Porter twitched, producing another gasp from Liz.

"We have no quarrel with the White Prophet," Snelgrove intervened. "The woman and her son are free to go, but at a cost. If they leave us, if they turn their back on the truly risen messiah, and on us, his transformed apostles, God knows what repercussions may rain down on them."

Martin stepped around Traveler and held a hand out toward Liz, but Porter shook his head. "She carries a child."

"Yours?" Martin asked.

"God's," Snelgrove answered, pointing a finger at Liz. "Tell your father that. Tell him you weren't touched against your will."

Porter relaxed his arm enough for her to speak.

"I promise," she croaked.

Traveler said, "Mrs. Smoot, you and your son go outside with my father."

At a nod from Snelgrove, Porter released her. She immediately scooped up the boy and retreated behind Martin, who half-turned to shepherd them out of the house.

"They are free," Porter said to Martin's back, "but you aren't." He swung the ax handle, catching Martin across the shoulders, just missing the back of his head.

Martin's cry was like an electric shock surging through Traveler's body. His muscles spasmed; his body lunged forward of its own accord.

The blow to his biceps had no effect, neither did the ax handle glancing off his forehead. His hands still found their target.

A fist grazed his ear, Hillman's maybe, though Traveler didn't really care. Another punch caught him in the rib cage, just above the spot Liz had worked on that first time at Shipler's. The pain fueled his rage, blinding him to everything but his attack on Orrin Porter.

A gun fired, Martin's .45 judging by the deafening roar of it, but Traveler held on.

A shouted "Moroni" replaced the ringing in Traveler's ears but his tunnel vision continued, with Porter at the end of it, distant, no longer fighting back.

"Moroni," Martin said more softly. "Please."

Traveler blinked, became aware of Martin touching his shoulder with one hand, his other hand clenching the .45.

"Moroni," Martin repeated, "don't kill him."

Traveler's hands came into focus. They were locked around Porter's throat. The man's eyes had rolled back in his head. His tongue protruded grotesquely.

The force of Traveler's attack had driven Porter against the wallboard. His legs were twitching, the beginning of a death dance.

Traveler opened his fingers and Porter collapsed onto the floor, gagging. Out of the corner of his eye, Traveler saw Snelgrove and Hillman cowering against the opposite wall. Liz had her son's face buried in the folds of her skirt.

The adrenaline flooded away, leaving Traveler weak in the knees. He touched his face and felt blood running from a gash in his forehead.

"Can you drive?" Martin said.

Traveler nodded, though the thought of the 250 miles to Provo and the BYU campus brought the ringing back to his ears.

From behind, Martin pushed him toward the door. Traveler hesitated at the threshold, part of him wanting to do more damage. Not for Martin's sake, but for Norm Shipler's, whose only crime had been to have two available daughters.

Traveler turned, made a finger gun and pantomimed a shot at each of the three self-appointed apostles, one after the other.

"Is that a threat?" Snelgrove asked.

"A promise," Traveler answered, "if anyone else in Fire Creek dies."

"What about natural causes?"

"If I were you, I'd hire a doctor to keep everyone healthy."

THIRTY-NINE

Three helicopters, large enough to be army troop carriers, stood on a playing field a quarter of a mile down the road from the BYU medical center. Even at that distance the men surrounding the choppers looked like soldiers wearing camouflage suits and bulky flak jackets. Only there were no military markings that Traveler could see.

"Danites," Martin observed. He and Traveler were sprawled on the bottom of a long flight of granite steps that led to the medical center. Martin was wearing a sling to take the pressure off his right shoulder, where Porter's ax handle had landed. The gash in Traveler's forehead had been closed temporarily with a bandage. Liz Smoot and young Josiah had already been rushed inside for further examination.

"Ellsworth's been a long time," Traveler said.

"He asked us to wait. Besides . . ." Without turning around, Martin jerked a thumb over his shoulder in the general direction of the Tongans who flanked the doorway, their muscled arms folded over fifty-inch chests. "They might bite."

It was Sunday morning, too early for BYU's summer school students to be in evidence. A light smelter haze hung over the campus and took the edge off the 11,000-foot Wasatch Front to the east, turning the granite peaks the color of old varnish.

The Tongans turned. By the time Traveler and Martin stood to face the building, the bodyguards were opening the glass doors. A moment later, Josiah Ellsworth strode across the threshold, his black suit and white dress shirt as immaculate as ever. He was accompanied by a man in a white lab coat, who stopped on the granite terrace to shake Ellsworth's hand, then cast a quick glance in Traveler's direction before retreating back inside.

At a nod from Ellsworth, the Tongans moved into position two paces behind him as he descended the steps. When he reached Traveler, he shook his hand formally, using a two-handed grip.

"I'm in your debt," he said. "When I heard my grandson was better, I thought it was only wishful thinking. Now that I've seen him for myself, I realize I should have had more faith. Of all people, I should know the power of prayer."

Ellsworth closed his eyes and lowered his head as if in silent communion. The Tongans never took their eyes off Traveler.

"Payment has already been transferred into your firm's account," Ellsworth said when he raised his head, "enough to cover any contingency, though I know better than to put a price on what you've done for me. One day, I'm sure, my grandson will want to thank you for himself. My daughter too."

He took Traveler's hand again and held on to it. "I don't know what Liz told you, or what you might have heard said about her conduct in Fire Creek. I take comfort in the fact that Willis Tanner assures me of your discretion, though I still feel it incumbent on me to set the record straight. There was never a pregnancy. That condition was pure hysteria on my daughter's part, probably the result of the strain of coping with young Josiah's illness. Any talk of intimacy outside of a church-sanctified marriage was sheer fantasy on her part. Maybe she was forced to say such things. Who

knows? We never will know probably. In any case, the doctors have assured me that my daughter was never in that condition. They have backed their diagnosis with signed affidavits."

Traveler stared into Ellsworth's eyes, wondering if the man actually believed what he was saying.

"May I count on your discretion?" Ellsworth asked, still clasping Traveler's hand.

"We were hired to find a messiah," Traveler said, "not make moral judgments."

Ellsworth released his grip. "I've found it best never to believe rumors, though at times they get the better of us, don't they. I plead guilty myself. I gave credence to foolish rumors, I sent you and your father into the desert on a wild goose chase." He shook his head. "Miracles. A messiah risen from the dead. I should have known better."

"They probably said the same thing in Judea two thousand years ago," Martin said.

Ellsworth grimaced. "We'd better have you seen to by the doctor. Where did you say that man Porter hit you, Brother Martin?"

"The shoulder, not the head."

"Judging by your son's condition, he wasn't so lucky."

"A glancing blow only," Traveler assured him.

"It's hard to say what can happen in the heat of battle," Ellsworth said. "You may be more seriously hurt than you think. Both of you may have concussions." He turned to one of the Tongans, snapped his fingers, and was immediately handed a palmsize two-way radio.

"This is Ellsworth," the apostle said into the radio.

"Standing by," came the reply.

"Everything is as reported. The woman and boy are safe."

Down the road, the men in camouflage suits began loading into the helicopters. Simultaneously, the engines coughed to life and the rotors swung into action.

"What the hell are you doing?" Traveler demanded, his tone

of voice triggering the Tongans, who instantly thrust themselves between him and Ellsworth.

Ellsworth smiled. "My daughter tells me there's no proof against these people. They call themselves Moroni's Children, a blasphemy in itself, and think they can get away with murder."

"We don't know who killed whom."

"At the least, you suspect them of killing a man named Shipler," Ellsworth replied. "Liz told me so. She said you were frustrated because you had nothing concrete."

The helicopters took off, one after the other, hovering momentarily over the playing field before heading south.

"Is that what you're after?" Martin said, pointing at the choppers. "Proof?"

"Think of it this way. Those cults are all guilty of something. They kill one another all the time, so innocence isn't really the point."

"What are their orders?" Traveler asked.

"Whose?"

"Your Danites."

Ellsworth looked south. The helicopters were distant dots in the sky. "I don't see anything, Mr. Traveler. Now, if you'll excuse me, I have work to do."

He spoke into the radio again and within moments, a silver limousine appeared in front of the medical center. Ellsworth opened the door himself, then hesitated. "My Tongan associates will escort you inside for treatment. Otherwise, you might be mistaken for Gentiles."

As soon as Traveler's forehead had been stitched and Martin's shoulder X-rayed, they were escorted to a top-floor suite. The doctor who opened the door was the same man who'd been talking to Ellsworth on the steps earlier. He nodded to the Tongans to stay where they were, then motioned Traveler and Martin inside.

"Thank you for coming," Liz Smoot said weakly from the bed where she lay propped against a stack of pillows. A plastic bag filled with an intravenous solution hung from a rack beside her, its clear solution dripping regularly into her wrist. Yet she looked so shrunken Traveler had the impression that the IV was window dressing only, that it was actually sucking away her vitality.

She tried to sit up but didn't have the strength, though she'd seemed well enough on the drive up from Fire Creek.

The doctor cranked up the head of her bed, which looked to be standard hospital issue. Everything else—sofas, chairs, the oriental rug, the paintings on the walls—had the opulence of an apostle's anteroom.

"You can't stay long," the doctor said to Traveler and Martin. "You shouldn't be here at all. Apostle Ellsworth was very clear about that."

"We've been all through that, Doctor," Liz said. "Otherwise, I press charges against the hospital for what you've done to me. Now, before you leave us alone, tell these gentlemen what you told my father."

The doctor looked at the door longingly. "Your son is fine, if that's what you mean. There's no sign of Hodgkin's disease."

"You told my father it was a miracle," she prompted. *"Miracle* was your word."

"Cases of spontaneous remission are not unknown," he said.

Liz wet her lips. "How often does that happen?"

"One in ten thousand, maybe less."

"You see," she said, nodding at Traveler and his father, "Jason Thurgood was the real thing. He cured my son."

"The original diagnosis could have been wrong," the doctor said.

Tears started down her cheeks. "It was made right here at this clinic. You know what I'm saying is the truth, that we're witnesses to a miracle. Now leave us alone."

"Your records show that you were admitted suffering from dehydration and extreme exhaustion," the man said before fleeing the room.

"They took my baby," she said once the door closed behind him. "I didn't know what they were doing. They gave me a shot and after that I just didn't have the strength to fight back. It was my father's doing. He told me that I was imagining things, that I wasn't really pregnant. That's why I asked to see you."

She held up her right arm, the one with the IV needle stuck into it. "God knows what's in here, so I'd better have my say quickly. They're all afraid, you know. They don't dare admit that the messiah has come again, and that once again we've murdered him. We're all of us murderers, my father included."

"Jason Thurgood wasn't what he seemed," Traveler said softly. "We've checked on him and—"

She cut him off. "We all have old sins. Jason confessed his to us."

"You heard his confession?"

"All of Moroni's Children did. We called a meeting and Jason got down on his knees. He told us he'd come among us to do penance. 'Called to do God's work,' Brother Snelgrove said, and we all agreed with him. We forgave Jason his sins as Christ would have forgiven ours."

"What sins?" Martin asked.

"For betraying his patients."

"Do you know who killed him?"

"Snelgrove's involved, I know that after what happened yesterday. At Earl's house, when they didn't think I could hear. I was in the bedroom as always, waiting for Orrin to . . . to perform his husbandly duties. But I had to go to the bathroom. While I was there, they moved into the kitchen and I could hear their voices through the heating vent. 'Someone saved us a murder,' Snelgrove said. 'Otherwise, we would have had to kill him ourselves.

You can't get anywhere in this business without a martyr.' "

"Does Snelgrove know who killed him?" Traveler held his breath, dreading the answer.

Sobs overwhelmed her. Martin sat beside her, feeding her fresh tissues.

"I'm as guilty as they are," she managed to say after a while. She clasped her belly through the thin hospital blanket. "God is punishing me already."

"Do *you* know who killed Jason?" Martin said.

She shook her head. "I know about Norm Shipler, though. Orrin bragged to me about it. It was the one time he didn't get someone else to do the dirty work for him." She shuddered. "We were in bed when he started laughing about it. 'I fucked the whole family, one way or another,' he said, 'just like I'm fucking you.' "

"Did you tell your father that?" Martin asked sharply.

"Yes, God help me."

FORTY

A hundred and ten degrees in downtown Salt Lake, an August record according to the radio, had South Temple Street's asphalt bubbling like black lava. In the Chester Building, the rising heat carried with it a stink of hot tar, as if roofers were at work overhead.

Traveler leaned back in his chair, propped his feet on the desk, and stared at the ceiling as if expecting to see hot pitch leaking through the seams. Across from him, Martin had assumed a similar position, only his eyes were closed and he was pretending to snore.

"We can't prove a damn thing," Traveler said. "Against anybody."

Martin snored louder.

"The miracle's to blame," Traveler said, trying without success to convince himself that some kind of justice had been done. "When word got to Ellsworth that the boy was cured, Jason Thurgood was as good as dead. Ruth took a picture of him at work and that was it. He was recognized for what he was.''

The phone rang.

"Your turn," Martin said. "I'm asleep."

Traveler hit the speaker phone. "Moroni Traveler and Son."

A woman said, "I have a collect call from Ottinger in Pioche, Nevada. Will you accept?"

Martin shook his head. Traveler said, "I'll accept the charges."

"This is Janet Ottinger, remember me?"

"Of course."

"You were looking for my husband, soon to be my ex."

Traveler eyed his father, who'd opened his eyes to a squint.

"We never did find him," Traveler said, figuring no one ever would now, without sifting through the ashes of Coffee Pot Springs.

"Well, I did. The bastard showed up last night, expecting me to take him back after a month-long drunk somewhere. 'No way,' I told him, but Jack wouldn't leave. He's passed out right in the middle of my living room rug, which I just had cleaned. So if you want him, come and get him. Take him away. Lock him up. Otherwise, I'm having the bastard arrested myself."

Martin came out of his chair to get closer to the speaker. "Did he say where he'd been?"

"He made up some cockamamie story. His job made him do it, he said. Getting drunk was the only way he could forget for a while what he'd done at that clinic of his. 'Bull to that,' I told him. 'You've been playing scientist for years and it never bothered you before. My guess is you've been off with some woman. Well, two can play that game, because as of next week the divorce will be final.' "

Martin muffled the speaker. "If Ottinger's alive, who the hell was Jason Thurgood?"

"Jack," she yelled, "someone wants to talk to you on the phone."

Traveler heard a groan in the background.

"It's long distance, for Christ's sake," she said. "A couple of detectives in Salt Lake, so get your butt over here without throwing up again."

"This is Jack Ottinger," a man said tentatively.

"My name's Moroni Traveler."

"We work for the Mormon Church," Martin added for leverage. "We were hired to find one of your patients, Petey Biscari."

"Tell me he's alive," Ottinger said.

Traveler said, "We found his body buried on the Indian reservation. The Indians say he didn't die from exposure. They say his hair fell out and he had vomiting and diarrhea."

"Christ."

"We represent his father," Martin said.

"You said you represented the church."

"Both."

Ottinger groaned again. "I can't comment on my patients."

"We can make your life hell," Traveler said.

"You bastards are FBI, aren't you? This is some kind of setup to test my loyalty."

"For Christ's sake, Jack," his wife said in the background. "You're getting paranoid again."

"What made the boy run away?" Martin asked.

When Ottinger didn't answer, Traveler said, "All right then, what made you run away?"

"I took a sabbatical."

Raising an eyebrow at Martin, Traveler said, "Just like Jason Thurgood?"

"Not at all. Thurgood . . . I knew it. This is some kind of counterintelligence security check, isn't it? Well, I know enough not to talk on the phone."

"Are you saying Thurgood worked for the clinic?"

"Without a lawyer, I'm saying nothing at all," Ottinger replied and hung up.

A minute later Mrs. Ottinger called again, this time on her own money. "Thank you, Mr. Traveler. I didn't have to bother throwing him out. Whatever you said to him sent him charging out of here like wolves were after him."

"The name Thurgood came up," Traveler said. "Does that mean anything to you."

"It sounds familiar."

"Dr. Jason Thurgood," he clarified.

"Mostly Jack talked about his patients. From the look on his face when he took off, I figured Thurgood was another one he must have lost. Are you coming after him?"

"We'll leave him to you."

"Sometimes I think lesbians have the right idea," she said and slammed down the receiver.

Martin shook his head. "If Thurgood worked for the government, we'll never know who he was."

"Do you think he cured Liz Smoot's boy?"

"You heard the doctor at BYU. With Hodgkin's disease, the odds for a spontaneous cure are ten thousand to one. That says to me the odds are in Thurgood's favor."

"I liked him," Traveler said.

Martin nodded. "He was haunted by demons, that's for sure. They drove him all the way to Fire Creek."

"From the clinic?"

"With Ottinger alive, it doesn't matter really. He's to blame for Petey. You know it and so do I. The only trouble is, old Petain didn't know it when he shot Thurgood."

Traveler's jaw dropped.

"For God's sake," Martin said. "I'm not senile yet and I'm not blind. Petain's footprints were all over the place, along with pawprints from that dog of his."

"I thought I erased them."

"Except for the ones you missed." Martin snorted. "Those, I rubbed out myself."

—

"I should have known better."

"You were keeping quiet for my benefit, I know that. What a man doesn't know, his conscience can't chew on. But now that the damage is done, we have to figure out what we're going to do about Petain."

"We have no actual proof against anyone," Traveler said.

"He's a good man, you know. If we tell him the truth, that he killed the wrong man, my guess is he'll give himself up to the police."

"Is that what you want?" Traveler said.

"Ellsworth hired us to find a messiah and rescue his daughter and grandson. As far as I'm concerned, we were successful all around. If one day, old Petain learns the truth, what happens then is up to him, not us. Do you agree?"

Traveler turned to the window, leaned his forehead against the hot glass, and stared at the temple across the street. Rising heat waves made it look like a mirage. "We should have known better than to go into cult country. It's downwind from hell."

FORTY-ONE

Barney Chester had installed a litter box and wicker basket behind the cigar stand in the Chester Building's lobby, though Brigham had yet to visit anything but Bill's lap.

"The ancient Egyptians had a cat god," Bill said, "so why can't I have a cat for an apostle?"

"Charlie will come back," Chester said.

"You weren't there, at the reservation, when he said goodbye." Bill shook his head. "No, my Church of the True Prophet is finished. No offence, Brigham"—he stroked the cat's ears—"but you can't have a church without human followers."

"You have us," Traveler said, speaking for himself and Martin.

Bill stared at them as if assessing the offer. "I'd need to baptize you."

Chester groaned.

"After that," Bill continued, warming to the idea, "we can take turns raising lost souls the way Charlie and I had planned.

What do you say, Barney, can we fill the font?''

The baptismal in question, an inflatable plastic wading pool, was serving as a protective ground sheet for Brigham's litter box.

"Tell us about Charlie," Chester said, in an obvious attempt to divert Bill. "Mo and Martin haven't heard the details yet."

Bill lowered his head, concentrating on Brigham's ears for a while. When he finally looked up, his eyes were filled with tears. "We were at the reservation raising souls, filling paradise with new followers, when suddenly, Charlie raises his hands to heaven and says, 'I must do more than this. I must help my people. The time has come for my great pilgrimage.' ''

Bill's rising voice caused Brigham to arch her back. " 'I will accompany you,' I told him. But no. Charlie said it was a journey he must make alone. I kept pace with him for miles, hoping he'd change his mind, until finally he told me he was walking all the way across the state. Two hundred miles, he said, all the way to the Navajo reservation. There, he told me, I would be the heathen. So I gave Charlie half our money, enough for him to take the bus.''

"And did he?'' Chester asked.

"I don't know. Mine came first. I've been praying for him ever since, alone in that desert.''

"Charlie's a survivor,'' Traveler said.

"We'd better baptize him first anyway.'' Bill began tugging at the flattened plastic pool. "We'll take turns blowing it up.''

Chester looked to Traveler and Martin for help. They were saved by the arrival of the Chester Building's elevator operator, Nephi Bates, who was waving the afternoon edition of the *Deseret News.*

"God's will be done.'' Bates slapped the paper down on the countertop hard enough to send Brigham skittering across the lobby's marble floor.

A front-page story, bylined Ruth Holcomb, told of a raid into southern Utah.

Sheriff's helicopters swooped down on the desert town of Fire Creek late yesterday seeking the killers of a young boy whose body was discovered in an unmarked grave during a lengthy undercover investigation.

"The boy was in the wrong place at the wrong time," said Don Miller, a spokesman for the Washington County Sheriff's Department. "He got caught in the middle between warring factions of an extremist religious cult calling itself Moroni's Children."

The victim, Petain Biscari, Jr., 16, had apparently wandered into the area accidentally, his father said when reached by phone.

Two of the cult leaders, tentatively identified as Horace Snelgrove and a man calling himself Orrin Porter, were among those killed resisting arrest during the massive helicopter assault.

Charges are pending against several others, whose names have not been released.

"There's no mention of the clinic, or its radiation experiments," Traveler said.

"What do you expect," Martin said. "The buck never stops anywhere. All bureaucrats have to do is wait. Sooner or later the downwind effect will kill off all the witnesses."

Traveler crushed the newspaper into a wad and hurled it halfway across the lobby. "My God, how I'd like to go after those responsible."

"Who? Harry Truman? He was president when they started testing those bombs. Or maybe Eisenhower? He was in office when they fired off Dirty Harry."

Bill dropped to his knees beside the wading pool. "I say we baptize that poor Biscari boy right now." He took a deep breath and blew into the inflation valve.

"Give it up," Chester said when Bill ran out of breath. "I bought you a pump."

When the pool was inflated and the water knee deep, Bill stripped to his underwear, then plunged his toes into the water. "This isn't going to work. I need Charlie. He was my proxy. He stood in for the dead while I prayed. And vice versa. A one-man church can't baptize the dead."

Chester rolled his eyes. "I'm your man."

"I must baptize you first, as I did Charlie."

With a sigh, Chester peeled off everything but his boxer shorts, then allowed himself to be dunked. When he came up for air, Bill said, "I pronounce you saved. Now"—Bill pushed him under again—"Petain Biscari is also raised."

Chester bobbed up, sputtering, "Who's next?"

"Like I've been saying," Bill said, "the Mormons have already grabbed Abe Lincoln and George Washington for themselves, so if we're going to attract new members to our church, we need some big names."

He looked at Martin. "What about the two you mentioned, Truman and Eisenhower?"

"No politicians," Traveler said. "Let them stay in hell where they belong."